THE TWO WIVES

OR, LOST AND WON

T. S. ARTHUR

1st WORLD
LIBRARY
Literary Society

The Two Wives

T. S. Arthur

© 1st World Library – Literary Society, 2004
PO Box 2211
Fairfield, IA 52556
www.1stworldlibrary.org
First Edition

LCCN: 2004195361

Softcover ISBN: 1-4218-0195-7
Hardcover ISBN: 1-4218-0095-0
eBook ISBN: 1-4218-0295-3

Purchase *"The Two Wives"*
as a traditional bound book at:
www.1stWorldLibrary.org/purchase.asp?ISBN=1-4218-0195-7

1st World Library Literary Society is a nonprofit
organization dedicated to promoting literacy by:

- Creating a free internet library accessible from any
  computer worldwide.
- Hosting writing competitions and offering book
  publishing scholarships.

The Two Wives
*contributed by Tim, Ed & Rodney
in support of
1st World Library Literary Society*

PREFACE

THE story of the "Two Wives; or, Lost and Won," is intended to show the power of tender, earnest, self-forgetting love, in winning back from the path of danger a husband whose steps have strayed, and who has approached the very brink of ruin; and, by contrast, to exhibit the sad consequences flowing from a want of these virtues under like circumstances.

This book is the third in the Series of "ARTHUR'S LIBRARY FOR THE HOUSEHOLD." The fourth, which is nearly ready, will be called "THE WAYS OF PROVIDENCE; OR, HE DOETH ALL THINGS WELL."

CHAPTER I

"YOU are not going out, John?" said Mrs. Wilkinson, looking up from the work she had just taken into her hands. There was a smile on her lips; but her eyes told, plainly enough, that a cloud was upon her heart.

Mrs. Wilkinson was sitting by a small work-table, in a neatly furnished room. It was evening, and a shaded lamp burned upon the table. Mr. Wilkinson, who had been reading, was standing on the floor, having thrown down his book and risen up hastily, as if a sudden purpose had been formed in his mind.

"I shall only be gone a little while, dear," returned Mr. Wilkinson, a slight air of impatience visible beneath his kind voice and manner.

"Don't go, John," said Mrs. Wilkinson, still forcing a smile to her countenance. "I always feel so lonely when you are away. We only have our evenings to be together; and I cannot bear then to be robbed of your company. Don't go out, John; that's a good, dear husband."

And Mrs. Wilkinson, in the earnestness of her desire to keep her husband at home, laid aside her sewing, and rising, approached and leaned her hands upon his shoulder, looking up with an affectionate, appealing expression into his face.

"You're a dear, good girl, Mary," said Mr. Wilkinson, tenderly, and he kissed the pure lips of his wife as he spoke. "I know it's wrong to leave you alone here. But, I won't be gone more than half an hour. Indeed I won't. See, now;" and he drew forth his watch; "it is just eight o'clock, and I will be home again precisely at half-past eight, to a minute."

Mrs. Wilkinson made no answer; but her husband saw that tears were in the eyes fixed so lovingly upon him.

"Now don't, love," said he, tenderly, "make so much of just half an hour's absence. I promised Elbridge that I would call around and see him about a little matter of business, and I must keep my word. I had forgotten the engagement until it crossed my mind while reading."

"If you have an engagement." There was a certain emphasis in the words of Mrs. Wilkinson that caused her husband to partly turn his face away.

"I have, dear. But for that, I should not think of leaving you alone."

Almost instinctively Mrs. Wilkinson withdrew the hands she had placed upon the shoulder of her husband, and receded from him a step or two; at the same time her face was bent downwards, and her eyes rested upon the floor.

For some moments Mr. Wilkinson stood as if in earnest debate with himself; then he said, in a cheerful, lively tone -

T. S. Arthur

"Good-by, love. I shall only be gone half an hour." And turning away, left the room. He did not pause until he was in the street. Then a spirit of irresolution came over him, and he said to himself, as he moved slowly away,

"It isn't kind in me to leave Mary alone in this way; I know it isn't. But I want to see Elbridge; and, in fact, partly promised that I would call upon him this evening. True, I can say all I wish to say to him in the morning, and to quite as good purpose. But -"

Wilkinson, whose steps had been growing more and more deliberate, stopped. For some time he stood, in a thoughtful attitude - then slowly returned. His hand was in his pocket, his dead-latch key between his fingers, and his foot upon the marble sill of his door. And thus he remained, in debate with himself, for as long a time as two or three minutes.

"Yes; I must see him! I had forgotten that," he exclaimed, in a low tone, and suddenly stepped back from the door, and with a rapid pace moved down the street. A walk of ten minutes brought him to the house of Mr. Elbridge. But it so happened that this gentleman was not at home.

"How soon do you expect him to return?" was inquired of the servant.

"He may be here in half an hour; or not before ten o'clock," was the reply.

Wilkinson was disappointed. Leaving his name with the servant, and saying that he would probably call again during the evening, he descended the steps and walked away. He was moving in the direction of his home, and had arrived within a block thereof when he stopped, saying to himself as he did so -

"I must see Elbridge this evening. It is already nearly half an hour since I left home, and I promised Mary that I would not remain away a moment longer than that time. But, I did not think Elbridge would be out. Poor Mary! She looks at me with such sad eyes, sometimes, that it goes to my very heart. She cannot bear to have me out of her sight. Can she doubt me in any thing? No; I will not believe that. She is a loving, gentle-minded creature - and one of the best of wives. Ah me! I wish I were more like her."

Still Wilkinson remained standing, and in debate with himself.

"I will go home," said he, at length, with emphasis, and walked quickly onward. He was within a few doors of his own home, when his steps began to linger again. He had come once more into a state of irresolution.

"Perhaps Elbridge has returned." This thought made him stop again. "He must have understood me that I would be around."

Just at this moment the crying of a child was heard.

"Is that Ella?" Wilkinson walked around a little way, until he came nearly opposite his own house. Then he stopped to listen more attentively.

Yes. It was the grieving cry of his own sick babe.

T. S. Arthur

"Poor child!" he murmured. "I wonder what can ail her?"

He looked up at the chamber windows. The curtains were drawn aside, and he saw upon the ceiling of the room the shadow of some one moving to and fro. He did not doubt that it was the shadow of his wife, as, with their sick babe in her arms, she walked to and fro in the effort to soothe it again to sleep. Had there been a doubt, it would have been quickly dispelled, for there came to his ears the soft tones of a voice he knew full well - came in tones of music, low and soothing, but with most touching sweetness. It was the voice of his wife, and she sang the air of the cradle-hymn with which he had been soothed to rest when he lay an innocent babe in his mother's arms.

The feelings of Wilkinson, a good deal excited by the struggle between affection and duty on the one side, and appetite and inclination on the other, were touched and softened by the incident, and he was about entering his house when the approaching form of a man, a short distance in advance, caught his eye, and he paused until he came up.

"Elbridge! The very one I wished to see!" he exclaimed, in a low voice, as he extended his hand and grasped that of his friend. "I've just been to your house. Did you forget that I was to call around?"

"I didn't understand you to say, certainly, that you would call, or I should have made it a point to be at home. But no matter. All in good time. I'm on my way home now, and you will please return with me."

"I don't know about that," said Wilkinson, who could

not forget his promise to his wife. "I told Mary, when I went out, that I would only be gone half an hour, and that time has expired already."

"Oh, never mind," returned the other, lightly. "She'll forgive you, I'll be bound. Tell her that you came home, in all obedience to her wishes, but that I met you at your own door, and carried you off in spite of yourself."

And as Elbridge said this, he drew his arm within that of Wilkinson, and the two men went chatting away.

Elbridge was fond of good wine, and always kept a few choice bottles on hand. Wilkinson knew this; and, if he had looked narrowly into his heart on the present occasion, he would have discovered that the wine of his friend had for him a stronger attraction than his company.

As the latter had anticipated, wine and cigars were produced immediately on their arrival at the house of Elbridge; and in the exhilaration of the one and the fumes of the other, he soon forgot his lonely, troubled wife and sick child at home.

A friend or two dropped in, in the course of half an hour; and then a second bottle of wine was uncorked, and glasses refilled with its sparkling contents.

The head of Wilkinson was not very strong. A single glass of wine generally excited him, and two or three proved, always, more than he could bear. It was so on this occasion; and when, at eleven o'clock, he passed forth from the house of his friend, it was only by an effort that he could walk steadily. The cool night air, as it breathed upon his heated brow, partially sobered him, and his thoughts turned towards his home. A sigh and the act of striking his hand upon his forehead marked the effect of this transition of thought.

"Poor Mary! I didn't mean to stay away so late. I meant to return in half an hour," he muttered, half aloud. "But this is always the way. I'm afraid I've taken too much of Elbridge's wine; a little affects me. I wonder if Mary will notice it; I wouldn't have her to do so for the world. Poor child! it would frighten her to death. I rather think I'd better try to walk off the effects of what I've been drinking. It's late, any how, and fifteen or twenty minutes will make but little difference either way."

As Wilkinson said this, he turned down a cross street which he happened to be passing at the moment, and moved along with a quicker pace. Gradually the confusion of his thoughts subsided.

"I wish I had remained at home," he sighed, as the image of his wife arose distinctly in his mind. "Poor Mary! I broke my word with her, though I promised so faithfully. Oh, dear! this weakness on my part is terrible. Why was I so anxious to see Elbridge? there was no real engagement, and yet I told Mary there was. I would not have her know of this deception for the world. I forgot about dear little Ella's being so sick; what if we should lose that little angel? Oh! I could not bear it!"

Wilkinson stopped suddenly as this thought flashed over his mind. He was soberer by far than when he left the house of Mr. Elbridge.

"I'll go home at once." He turned and began quickly retracing his steps. And now he remembered the moving shadow on the wall, as he stood, nearly three hours before, in front of his house, debating with himself whether to enter or no. He heard too, in imagination, the plaintive cries of his sick child, and the soothing melody of its mother's voice as she sought to hush into sleep its unquiet spirit.

CHAPTER II

WILKINSON was nearly in front of his own door, when he was thus familiarly accosted by a man named Ellis, who came leisurely walking along with a lighted cigar in his mouth.

"Hallo! is this you, Wilkinson? What in the name of wonder are you doing out at such an hour?"

"And suppose I were to ask you the same question?" inquired Wilkinson, as he took the hand of the other, who was an old acquaintance.

"It would be easily answered," was the unhesitating reply of Ellis, who had been drinking rather freely.

"Well, suppose I have the benefit of your answer."

"You're quite welcome. I keep no secrets from an old friend, you see. Can't you guess?"

"I'm not good at guessing."

"Had a little tiff with Cara," said Ellis in a half whisper, as he bent to the ear of his companion.

"Oh, no!" returned Wilkinson.

"Fact. Cara's a dear, good soul, as you know; but she's a self-willed little jade, and if I don't do just as she wants me to - if I don't walk her chalk line - *presto!* she goes off like a rocket. To-night, d'ye see, I came home with the first volume of Prescott's new work on Mexico - a perfect romance of a book, and wanted to read it aloud to Cara. But no, she had something else in her head, and told me, up and down, that she didn't want to hear any of my dull old histories. I got mad, of course; I always get mad when she comes athwart my hawes in this way.

"'Dull old histories!' said I, indignantly. 'There's more true life and real interest in this book than in all the Wandering Jews or Laura Matilda novels that ever were written; and I wish you'd throw such miserable trash into the fire, and read books from which to get some intelligence and strength of mind.' Whew! The way she combed my hair for me at this was curious. I am a philosopher, and on these occasions generally repeat to myself the wise saw -

'He that fights and runs away,
May live to fight another day.'

So, deeming discretion the better part of valour, I retreated in disorder."

"That's bad," remarked Wilkinson, who knew something of the character of his friend's wife.

"I know it's bad; but, then, I can't help myself. Cara has such a queer temper, I never know how to take her."

"You ought to understand her peculiarities by this time, and bear with them."

T. S. Arthur

"Bear with them! I'd like to see you have the trial for a while; your wife is an angel. Ah, John! you're a lucky dog. If I had such a sweet-tempered woman in my house, I would think it a very paradise."

"Hush! hush! Harry; don't speak in that way. Few women possess so many good qualities as Mrs. Ellis; and it is your duty to cherish and love the good, and to bear with the rest."

"Well preached; but, as I am to apply the discourse, and not you, I must beg to be excused."

"Good-night. Go home, kiss Cara, and forgive her," said Wilkinson; and he made a motion to pass on, adding, as he did so, "I'm out much later than usual, and am in a hurry to get back. Mary will be uneasy about me."

But Ellis caught hold of one of his arms with both hands, and held on to him.

"Can't let you go, Wilkinson" said he, firmly. You're the man of all others I want to see - been thinking about you all the evening; want to have a long talk with you."

"Any other time, but not now," replied Wilkinson.

"Now, and no other time," persisted the other, clinging fast to his arm.

"What do you wish to talk about?" said Wilkinson, ceasing his effort to release himself from the firm grip of his friend.

"About Cara," was answered.

"Go home and make it up with her; that's the best way. She loves you, and you love her; and your love will settle all differences. And besides, Harry, you shouldn't talk about these things to other people. The relation between man and wife is too sacred for this."

"Do you think I talk in this way to everybody? No, indeed!" responded Ellis, in a half-offended tone of voice. "But you're a particular friend. You know Cara's peculiar temper, and can advise with me as a friend. So come along, I want to have a talk with you."

"Come where?"

Ellis turned and pointed to a brilliant gas lamp in the next square, that stood in front of a much frequented tavern.

"No, no; I must go home." And Wilkinson tried to extricate himself from the firm grasp of his friend. But the latter tightened his hold, as he said -

"It's of no use. I shall not let you go. So come along with me to Parker's. Over a couple of brandy toddies we will discuss this matter of Cara's."

A vigorous jerk from the hand of Ellis gave the body of Wilkinson a motion in the direction of the tavern. Had his mind been perfectly clear - had none of the effects of his wine-drinking at Elbridge's remained, he would have resisted to the end this solicitation, at the hour and under the circumstances. But his mind was not perfectly clear. And so, a few steps being taken by compulsion, he moved on by a sort of

T. S. Arthur

constrained volition.

As mentioned above, Wilkinson had nearly reached his own door when he encountered Ellis; was, in fact, so near, that he could see the light shining from the chamber-window through which, some hours before, he had marked on the wall the flitting shadow of his wife, as she walked to and fro, seeking to soothe into slumber her sick and grieving child. For nearly five minutes, he had stood talking with his friend, and the sound of their voices might easily have been heard in his dwelling, if one had been listening intently there. And one was listening with every sense strung to the acutest perception. Just as Wilkinson moved away, an observer would have seen the door of his house open, and a slender female form bend forth, and look earnestly into the darkness. A moment or two, she stood thus, and then stepped forth quickly, and leaning upon the iron railing of the door steps, fixed eagerly her eyes upon the slowly receding forms of the two men.

"John! John!" she called, in half suppressed tones.

But her voice did not reach the ear of her husband, whose form she well knew, even in the obscurity of night.

Gliding down the steps, Mrs. Wilkinson ran a few paces along the pavement, but suddenly stopped as some thought passed through her mind; and, turning, went back to the door she had left. There she stood gazing after her husband, until she saw him enter the tavern mentioned as being kept by a man named Parker, when, with a heavy, fluttering sigh, she passed into the house, and ascended to the chamber from which she had, a few minutes before, come down.

It was past eleven o'clock. The two domestics had retired, and Mrs. Wilkinson was alone with her sick child. Ella's moan of suffering came on her ear the instant she re-entered the room, and she stepped quickly to the crib, and bent over to look into its face. The cheeks of the child were flushed with fever to a bright crimson, and she was moving her head from side to side, and working her lips as if there was something in her mouth. Slight twitching motions of the arms and hands were also noticed by the mother. Her eyes were partly open.

"Will Ella have a drink of water?" said Mrs. Wilkinson, placing her hand under the child's head, and slightly raising it from the pillow.

But Ella did not seem to hear.

"Say - love, will you have some water?"

There was no sign that her words reached the child's ears.

A deeper shade of trouble than that which already rested on the mother's face glanced over it.

"Ella! Ella!" Mrs. Wilkinson slightly shook the child.

The only response was the muttering of some incoherent words, and a continued moaning as if pain were disturbing her sleep.

The mother now bent low over her child, and eagerly marked the expression of her face and the character of

T. S. Arthur

her breathing. Then she laid a hand upon her cheek. Instantly it was withdrawn with a quick start, but as quickly replaced again.

"What a burning fever!" she murmured. Then she added, in a tone of anxiety,

"How strangely she works her mouth! I don't like this constant rolling of her head. What can it mean? Ella! Ella!"

And she shook the child again.

"Want some water, love?"

The mother's voice did not appear to reach the locked sense of hearing.

Mrs. Wilkinson now lifted a glass of water from the bureau near by, and raising the head of Ella with one hand, applied, with the other, the water to her lips. About a table-spoonful was poured into her mouth. It was not swallowed, but ran out upon the pillow.

"Mercy! mercy! what can ail the child!" exclaimed Mrs. Wilkinson, a look of fear coming into her face.

A little while she stood over her, and then leaving her place beside the crib, she hurried out into the passage, and, pausing at the bottom of the stairs leading to the room above, called several times -

"Anna! Anna! Anna!"

But no answer came. The domestic thus summoned had fallen into her first sound sleep, and the voice did not penetrate her ears.

"Anna!" once more called Mrs. Wilkinson.

There was no response, but the reverberation of her own voice returned upon the oppressive silence. She now hurried back to her sick child, whose low, troubled moaning had not been hushed for a moment.

There was no apparent change. Ella lay with her half-opened eyes, showing, by the white line, that the balls were turned up unnaturally; with her crimsoned cheeks, and with the nervous motions of her lips and slight twitchings of her hands, at first noticed with anxiety and alarm.

Mrs. Wilkinson was but little familiar with sickness in children; and knew not the signs of real danger - or, rather, what unusual signs such as those now apparent in Ella really indicated. But she was sufficiently alarmed, and stood over the child, with her eyes fixed eagerly upon her.

Again she tried to arouse her from so strange and unnatural a state, but with as little effect as at first.

"Oh, my husband!" she at length exclaimed, clasping her hands together, and glancing upward, with tearful eyes, "why are you away from me now? Oh, why did you break your promise to return hours and hours ago?"

Then covering her face with her hands, she sobbed and wept, until, startled by a sharp, unnatural cry from the lips of Ella, her attention was once more fixed upon her suffering child.

T. S. Arthur

CHAPTER III

"Now, what will you take?" said Henry Ellis, as he entered, with the weak and yielding Wilkinson, the bar-room of Parker's tavern.

"Any thing you choose to call for," replied Wilkinson, whose mind was turning homeward, and who wished to be there. "In fact, I don't really want any thing. Call for two glasses of cold water. These will leave our heads clear."

"Water! Ha! ha! That is a good one, Bill" - and Ellis spoke to the bar-tender - "Mix us a couple of stiff brandy toddies."

The bar-tender nodded and smiled his acceptance of the order, and the two men retired to a table that stood in a remote part of the room, at which they were soon served with the liquor.

"Bill mixes the best brandy toddy I ever tasted. He knows his business," said Ellis, as he put the glass to his lips. "Isn't it fine?"

"It is very good," replied Wilkinson, as he sipped the tempting mixture.

But his thoughts were turning homeward, and he

scarcely perceived the taste of what he drank. Suddenly, he pushed the glass from him, and, making a motion to rise from the table, said -

"Indeed, Ellis, I must go home. My child is sick, and Mary will be distressed at my absence. Come around to my store, to-morrow, and we will talk this matter over. Neither you nor I are now in a fit state to discuss so grave a matter.

" Sit down, will you!"

This was the reply of Ellis, as he caught quickly the arm of his friend, and almost forced him, by main strength, to resume his seat.

"There, now," he added, as Wilkinson resumed his seat. "Never put off until to-morrow what can as well be done to-day. That is my motto. I want to talk with you about Cara, and no time is so good as the present."

"Well, well," returned Wilkinson, impatiently. "What do you want to say? Speak quickly, and to the point."

"Just what I'm going to do. But, first, I must see the bottom of my tumbler. There, now; come, you must do the same. Drink to good old times, and eternal friendship - drink, my fast and faithful friend!"

The warmth of the room and the quick effects of a strong glass of brandy toddy were making rapid advances on Ellis's partial state of inebriety.

Wilkinson emptied his glass, and then said -

"Speak, now, I'm all attention."

"Well, you see, Jack," and Ellis leaned over towards Wilkinson familiarly, and rested his arm upon his knee. You see, Jack, that huzzy of mine - if I must call the dear girl by such a name - is leading me the deuce of a life. Confound her pretty face! I love her, and would do almost any thing to please her; but she won't be pleased at any thing. She combs my head for me as regularly as the day comes."

"Hush - hush! Don't talk so of Cara. Her temper may be a little uncertain, but that is her weakness. She is your wife, and you must bear with these things. It isn't manly in you to be vexed at every trifle."

Trifle! Humph! I'd like you to have a week of my experience. You wouldn't talk any more about trifles."

"You should humour her a great deal, Harry. I am not so sure that you are not quite as much to blame for these differences and fallings out as she is."

" I wasn't to blame to-night, I am sure. Didn't I bring home Prescott, thinking that she would be delighted to have me sit the evening with her and read so charming an author? But, at the very proposition, she flared up, and said she didn't want to hear my musty old histories. Humph! A nice way to make a man love his home. Better for her and me, too, I'm thinking, that she had listened to the history, and kept her husband by her side."

"And for me, too," thought Wilkinson. "I should now, at least, be at home with my loving-hearted wife. Ah, me!"

"Now, what am I to do, Jack - say? Give me

your advice."

"The first thing for you to do is to go home, and to go at once. Come!"

And Wilkinson made another effort to rise; but the hand of Ellis bore him down.

"Stay, stay!" he muttered, impatiently. "Now don't be in such a confounded hurry. Can't you talk with an old friend for a minute or so? Look here, I've been thinking - let me see - what was I going to say?"

The mind of Ellis was growing more and more confused; nor was the head of Wilkinson so clear as when he entered the bar-room. The strong glass of brandy toddy was doing its work on both of them.

"Let me see," went on Ellis, in a wandering way. I was speaking of Cara - oh, yes, of Cara. Bless her heart, but confound her crooked temper! Now, what would you advise me to do, my old friend?"

"Go home, I have said," replied Wilkinson.

"And get my head combed with a three-legged stool? No, blast me if I do! I've stayed out this long just to make her sensible of her unkindness to one of the best of husbands - and I'm not going home until I am dead drunk. I guess that'll bring her to her bearings. Ha! Don't you think so, Jack?"

"Good heavens!" was just at this instant exclaimed by one of the inmates of the bar-room, in a low, startled tone of voice.

T. S. Arthur

"Your wife, as I live!" fell from the lips of Ellis, whose face was turned towards the entrance of the bar-room.

Wilkinson sprang to his feet. Just within the door stood a female form, her head uncovered, her under person clad in a white wrapper, and her face colourless as the dress she wore. There was a wild, frightened look in her staring eyes.

"Is Mr. Wilkinson here?" she asked, just as her husband's eyes rested upon her, and her thrilling voice reached his ears.

With a bound, Wilkinson was at her side.

"Oh, John! John!" she cried, in a voice of anguish. "Come home! Come quick! Our dear little Ella is dying!"

An instant more, and, to the inmates of the bar-room, the curtain fell upon that startling scene; for Wilkinson and his wife vanished almost as suddenly as if they had sunk together through the floor.

CHAPTER IV

DURING the day on which our story opened, Henry Ellis had obtained from a friend the first volume of Prescott's History of Mexico, then just from the press. An hour's perusal of its fascinating pages awakened in his mind a deep interest.

"Just the book to read to Cara," said he to himself, closing the volume, and laying it aside. "She's too much taken up with mere fiction. But here is that truth which is stranger than fiction; and I am sure she will soon get absorbed in the narrative."

With his new book, and this pleasant thought in his mind, Ellis took his way homeward, after the business of the day was over. As he walked along, a friend overtook him, and said, familiarly, as he touched him on the shoulder,

"I'm glad to overhaul you so opportunely. Half a dozen times, to-day, I have been on the eve of running round to see you, but as often was prevented. All in good time yet, I hope. I want you to come over to my room, this evening. There are to be three or four of our friends there, and some good eating and drinking into the bargain."

"A temptation certainly," replied Ellis. "No man likes

T. S. Arthur

good company better than I do; but, I rather think I must forego the pleasure this time."

"Why do you say that?"

I've promised myself another pleasure."

"Another engagement?"

"Not exactly that. Barker has loaned me the first volume of Prescott's Mexico; and I'm going to spend the evening in reading it to my wife."

"Any other evening will do as well for that," returned the friend. "So promise me to come around. I can't do without you."

"Sorry to disappoint you," said Ellis, firmly. "But, when I once get my mind fixed on a thing, I am hard to change."

"Perhaps your wife may have some engagement on hand, for the evening, or be disinclined for reading. What then?"

"You will see me at your room," was the prompt answer of Ellis; and the words were uttered with more feeling than he had intended to exhibit. The very question brought unpleasant images before his mind.

"I shall look for you," said the friend, whose name was Jerome. Good evening!"

"Good evening! Say to your friends, if I should not be there, that I am in better company."

The two men parted, and Ellis kept on his way homeward. Not until the suggestion of Jerome that his wife might be disinclined to hear him read, did a remembrance of Cara's uncertain temper throw a shade across his feelings. He sighed as he moved onward.

"I wish she were kinder and more considerate," he said to himself. "I know that I don't always do right; yet, I am not by any means so bad as she sometimes makes me out. To any thing reasonable, I am always ready to yield. But when she frowns if I light a cigar; and calls me a tippler whenever she detects the smell of brandy and water, I grow angry and stubborn. Ah, me!"

Ellis sighed heavily. A little way he walked on, and then began communing with himself.

"I don't know" - he went on - "but, may be, I do take a little too much sometimes. I rather think I must have been drinking too freely when I came home last week: by the way Cara talked, and by the way she acted for two or three days afterwards. There may be danger. Perhaps there is. My head isn't very strong; and it doesn't take much to affect me. I wish Cara wouldn't speak to me as she does sometimes. I can't bear it. Twice within the last month, she has fairly driven me off to spend my evening in a tavern, when I would much rather have been at home. Ah, me! It's a great mistake. And Cara may find it out, some day, to her sorrow. I like a glass of brandy, now and then; but I'm not quite so far gone that I must have it whether or no. I'm foolish, I will own, to mind her little, pettish, fretful humours. I ought to be more of a man than I am. But, I didn't make myself, and can't help feeling annoyed, and sometimes angry, when she is unkind and unreasonable. Going off to a tavern don't mend the matter, I'll admit; but, when I leave the house, alone, after nightfall, and in a bad humour, it is the most natural thing in the world for me to seek the pleasant company of some of my old friends - and I generally know where to find them."

Such was the state of mind in which Ellis returned home.

A word or two will give the reader a better idea of the relation which Henry Ellis and his wife bore to each other and society. They had been married about six years, and had three children, the oldest a boy, and the other two girls. Ellis kept a retail dry-goods store, in a small way. His capital was limited, and his annual profits, therefore, but light. The consequence was, that, in all his domestic arrangements, the utmost frugality had to be observed. He was a man of strict probity, with some ambition to get ahead in the world. These made him careful and economical in his expenditures, both at home and in the management of his business. As a man, he was social in his feelings, but inclined to be domestic. While unmarried, he had lived rather a gay life, and formed a pretty large acquaintance among young men. His associations led him into the pretty free use of intoxicating drinks; but the thought of becoming a slave of a vicious appetite never once crossed his mind with its warning shadow.

The first trial of Henry Ellis's married life was the imperative necessity that required him to lay a restraining hand upon his wife's disposition to spend money more freely than was justified by their circumstances. He had indulged her for the period of a whole year, and the result was so heavy a balance against his expense account, that he became anxious and troubled. There must be a change, or his business would be crippled, and ultimate ruin follow. As gently as he could, Ellis brought the attention of his wife to this matter. But, she could not comprehend, to its full extent, the point he urged. It then became necessary for Ellis to hold the purse-strings more tightly than he had formerly done. This fretted the mind of his wife, and often led her, in the warmth of the moment of disappointment, to utter unkind expressions. These hurt Ellis; and, sometimes, made him angry. The cloud upon Cara's brow, consequent upon these occasional misunderstandings, was generally so unpleasant to Ellis, whose heart was ever wooing the sunshine, let the rays come through almost any medium, that he would spend his evenings abroad. Temptation, as a natural consequence, was in his way. His convivial character made him seek the company of those who do not always walk the safest paths. How anxious should be the wife of such a husband to keep him at home; how light the task would have been for Cara. Alas! that she was so selfish, so self-willed - so blind! The scene that occurred on the evening of Ellis's return home with the book he wished to read for his wife, will give a fair view of Mrs. Ellis's manner of reacting upon her husband; and his mode of treating her on such occasions.

It has been seen in what state of feeling the husband returned home. Remembrances of the past brought some natural misgivings to his mind. His face, therefore, wore rather a more subdued expression than usual. Still, he was in a tolerably cheerful frame of mind - in fact, he was never moody. To his great relief, Cara met him with a smile, and seemed to be in an unusually good humour. Their sweet babe was lying asleep on her lap; and his other two children were

T. S. Arthur

playing about the room. Instantly the sunshine fell warmly again on the heart of Ellis. He kissed mother and children fervently, and with a deep sense of love.

"I called to see the bride this afternoon," said Mrs. Ellis, soon after her husband came in.

"Ah, did you?" he answered. "At her new home?"

"Yes."

"She is well and happy, of course?"

"Oh, yes; happy as the day is long. How could she help being so in such a little paradise?"

"Love makes every spot a paradise," said Ellis.

"Beg your pardon," replied the wife, with some change in her tone of voice. "I'm no believer in that doctrine. I want something more than love. External things are of account in the matter; and of very considerable account."

"They have every thing very handsome, of course," said Ellis; who was generally wise enough not to enter into a discussion with his wife on subjects of this kind.

"Oh, perfect!" replied his wife, "perfect! I never saw a house furnished with so much taste. I declare it has put me half out of conceit with things at home. Oh, dear! how common every thing did look when I returned."

"You must remember that our furniture has been in use for about six years," said Ellis; "and, moreover, that it was less costly than your friend's, in the beginning.

Her husband and your's are in different circumstances."

"I know all about that," was returned, with a toss of the head. "I know that we are dreadfully poor, and can hardly get bread for our children."

"We are certainly not able to furnish as handsomely as Mr. and Mrs. Beaumont. There is no denying that, Cara. Still, we are able to have every real comfort of life; and therewith let us try to be content. To desire what we cannot possess, will only make us unhappy."

"You needn't preach to me," retorted Mrs. Ellis, her face slightly flushing. "When I want to hear a sermon, I'll go to church."

Mr. Ellis made no answer, but, lifting his babe from its mother's lap, commenced tossing it in the air and singing a pleasant nursery ditty. Caroline sat in a moody state of mind for some minutes, and then left the room to give some directions about tea. On her return, Ellis said, in as cheerful a voice as if no unpleasant incident had transpired,

"Oh! I had forgotten to say, Cara, that Mr. Hemming and his wife have returned from Boston. They will be around to see us some evening this week."

"Hum-m - well." This was the cold, moody response of Mrs. Ellis.

"Mr. Hemming says that his wife's health is much better than it was."

"Does he?" very coldly uttered.

"He seemed very cheerful."

Mrs. Ellis made no comment upon this remark of her husband, and the latter said nothing more.

Tea was soon announced, and the husband and wife went, with their two oldest children, to partake of their evening meal. A cloud still hung over Caroline's features. Try as Ellis would to feel indifferent to his wife's unhappy state of mind, his sensitiveness to the fact became more and more painful every moment. The interest at first felt in his children, gradually died away, and, by the time supper was over, he was in a moody and fretted state, yet had he manfully striven to keep his mind evenly balanced.

On returning to the sitting-room, the sight of the book he had brought home caused Ellis to make a strong effort to regain his self-possession. He had set his heart on reading that book to Cara, because he was sure she would get interested therein; and he hoped, by introducing this better class of reading, to awaken a healthier appetite for mental food than she now possessed. So he occupied himself with a newspaper, while his wife undressed the children and put them to bed. It seemed to him a long time before she was ready to sit down with her sewing at the table, upon which the soft, pleasant light of their shaded lamp was falling. At last she came, with her small work-basket in her mind. Topmost of all its contents was a French novel. When Ellis saw this, there came doubts and misgivings across his heart.

"Cara," said he quickly, and in a tone of forced cheerfulness, taking up, at the same time, his volume of Prescott, - "I brought this book home on purpose to read aloud. I dipped into it, to-day, and found it so exceedingly interesting, that I deferred the pleasure of its perusal until I could share it with you."

Now, under all the circumstances, it cost Ellis considerable effort to appear cheerful and interested, while saying this.

"What book is it?" returned Cara, in a chilling tone, while her eyes were fixed upon her husband's face, with any thing but a look of love.

"The first volume of Prescott's History of Mexico, one of the most charming" -

"Pho! I don't want to hear your dull old histories!" said Cara, with a contemptuous toss of the head.

"Dull old histories!" retorted Ellis, whose patience was now gone. "Dull old histories! You don't know what you are talking about. There's more real interest in this book than in all the French novels that ever were invented to turn silly women's heads."

Of course, Mrs. Ellis "fired up" at this. She was just at the right point of ignition to blaze out at a single breath of reproof. We will not repeat the cutting language she used to her husband. Enough, that, in the midst of the storm that followed, Ellis started up, and bowing, with mock ceremony, said -

"I wish you good evening, madam. And may I see you in a better humour when we meet again."

A moment afterwards, and Caroline was alone with her own perturbed feelings and unpleasant, self-rebuking thoughts. Still, she could not help muttering, as a kind of justification of her own conduct -

"A perfect Hotspur! It's rather hard that a woman can't speak to her husband, but he must fling himself off in this way. Why didn't he read his history, if it was so very interesting, and let me alone. I don't care about such things, and he knows it."

After this, Mrs. Ellis fell into a state of deep and gloomy abstraction of mind. Many images of the past came up to view, and, among them, some that it was by no means pleasant to look upon. This was not the first time that her husband had gone off in a pet; but in no instance had he come home with a mind as clear as when he left her. A deep sigh heaved the wife's bosom as she remembered this; and, for some moments, she suffered from keen self-reproaches. But, an accusing spirit quickly obliterated this impression. In her heart she wrote many bitter things against her husband, and magnified habits and peculiarities into serious faults.

Poor, unhappy wife! How little did she comprehend the fact that her husband's feet were near the brink of a precipice, and that a fearful abyss of ruin was below; else would she have drawn him lovingly back, instead of driving him onward to destruction.

CHAPTER V

ELLIS, excited and angry, not only left his wife's presence, but the house. Repulsed by one pole, he felt the quick attraction of another. Not a moment did he hesitate, on gaining the street, but turned his steps toward the room of Jerome, where a party of gay young men were to assemble for purposes of conviviality.

We will not follow him thither, nor describe the manner of his reception. We will not picture the scene of revelry, nor record the coarse jests that some of the less thoughtful of the company ventured to make on the appearance of Ellis in their midst - for, to most of his friends, it was no secret that his wife's uncertain temper often caused him to leave his home in search of more congenial companionship. Enough, that at eleven o'clock, Ellis left the house of Jerome, much excited by drink.

The pure, cool night air, as it bathed the heated temples of Henry Ellis, so far sobered him by the time he reached his own door, that a distant remembrance of what had occurred early in the evening was present to his thoughts; and, still beyond this, a remembrance of how he had been received on returning at a late hour in times gone by. His hand was in his pocket, in search of his dead-latch key, when he suddenly retreated from

T. S. Arthur

the door, muttering to himself -

"I'm not going to stand a curtain lecture! There now! I'll wait until she's asleep."

Saying which, he drew a cigar and match-box from his pocket, and lighting the former, placed it between his lips, and moved leisurely down the street.

The meeting with Wilkinson has already been described.

Scarcely less startled was Ellis at the sudden apparition of Mrs. Wilkinson than her husband had been. He remained only a few moments after they retired. Then he turned his steps again homeward, with a clearer head and heavier heart than when he refused to enter, in fear of what he called a "curtain lecture."

Many painful thoughts flitted through his mind as he moved along with a quick pace.

"I wish Cara understood me better, or that I had more patience with her," he said to himself. "This getting angry with her, and going off to drinking parties and taverns is a bad remedy for the evil, I will confess. It is wrong in me, I know. Very wrong. But I can't bear to be snapped, and snubbed up, and lectured in season and out of season. I'm only flesh and blood. Oh dear! I'm afraid evil will come of it in the end. Poor Wilkinson! What a shock the appearance of his wife must have given him! It set every nerve in my body to quivering. And it was all my fault that he wasn't at home with his watching wife and sick child. Ah me! How one wrong follows another!"

Ellis had reached his own door. Taking out his night-key, he applied it to the latch; but the door did not open. It had been locked.

"Locked out, ha!" he ejaculated quickly; and with a feeling of anger. His hand was instantly on the bell-pull, and he jerked it three or four times vigorously; the loud and continued ringing of the bell sounding in his ears where he stood on the doorstep without. A little while he waited, and then the ringing was renewed, and with a more prolonged violence than at first. Then he listened, bending his ear close to the door. But he could detect no movement in the house.

"Confound it!" came sharp and impatiently from his lips. "If I thought this was designed, I'd -"

He checked himself, for just at that instant he saw a faint glimmer of light through the glass over the door. Then he perceived the distant shuffle of feet along the passage floor. There was a fumbling at the key and bolts, and then the half-asleep and half-awake servant admitted him.

"I didn't know you was out, sir," said the servant, "or I wouldn't have locked the door when I went to bed."

Ellis made no reply, but entered and ascended to his chamber. Cara was in bed and asleep, or apparently so. Her husband did not fail to observe a certain unsteady motion of the lashes that lay over her closed eyes; and he was not far wrong in his impression that she was awake, and had heard his repeated ringing for admission. His belief that such was the case did not lessen the angry feelings produced by the fact of having the key of his own door turned upon him.

T. S. Arthur

But slumber soon locked his senses into oblivion, and he did not awake until the sun was an hour above the horizon.

The moment Mrs. Wilkinson emerged, with her husband, from the bar-room of Parker's tavern, she fled along the street like a swift gliding spirit, far outstripping in speed her thoroughly sobered and alarmed husband, who hurried after her with rapid steps. The door of the house had been left open when she came forth in the anguish of her wild alarm to summon her husband, and she re-entered and flew up-stairs without the pause of an instant. Wilkinson was but a moment or two later in reaching the house, and in gaining their chamber. The sight that met his eyes sent the blood coldly to his heart. The mother had already snatched the child from the crib in which she had left her, and was standing with her close to the lamp, the light from which fell strongly upon her infantile face, that was fearfully distorted. The eyes were open and rolled up, until the entire pupil was hidden. The lips were white with their firm compression; and yet they had a quick nervous motion.

"Oh, John! John! what is the matter?" cried Mrs. Wilkinson, as she looked first upon the face of her child, and then into that of her husband, with a most anxious and imploring glance. "Is she dying?"

"No, dear, I think not," returned Wilkinson, with a composure of voice that belied the agitation of his feelings.

"Oh! what is the matter? Yes! Yes! I'm sure she's dying. Oh! run quick! quick! for the doctor."

"First," said Wilkinson, who was becoming, every moment, more self-possessed, and who now saw that the child, who was teething, had been thrown into spasms, "let us do what we can for her. She is in convulsions, and we must get her into a bath of hot water as quickly as possible. I will call up Anna. Don't be alarmed," he added, in a soothing voice: "there is no immediate danger."

"Are you sure, John? Are you sure? Oh! I'm afraid she is dying! My precious, precious babe!" And the mother clasped her child passionately to her bosom.

In the course of ten or fifteen minutes, a vessel of hot water was ready, and into this the still writhing form of the convulsed child was placed. Then Wilkinson hurried off for their physician. Half an hour afterwards he returned with him. The good effects of the hot-bath were already perceptible. The face of the child had resumed its placid sweetness of expression, and there was but slight convulsive twitching in the limbs. The doctor remained with them, applying, from time to time, appropriate remedies, until all the painful signs which occasioned so much alarm had vanished, and then left, promising to call early on the next morning.

It was past one o'clock. The physician had left, and the domestics retired to their own apartment. Mr. and Mrs. Wilkinson were alone with their still unconscious child, that lay in a deep, unnatural slumber. They were standing, side by side, and bending over the bed on which little Ella lay. Wilkinson had drawn his arm around his wife, and she had laid her head upon his shoulder. Each heard the beating of the other's heart, as thus they stood, silent, yet with troubled thoughts and oppressed feelings.

T. S. Arthur

A tear fell upon the hand of Wilkinson, and the warm touch, coming as it did in that moment of intense excitement, caused a quick thrill to pass through his nerves; and he started involuntarily. Words of confession and promises for the future were on his tongue; but, their utterance, just at that moment, seemed untimely, and he merely answered the mute appeal of tears with a fervent, heart-warm kiss, that, if the power of his will could have gone with it, would have filled the heart of his wife with joy unspeakable. Scarcely had his lips touched hers, ere she started up, and flung her arms around his neck, sobbing -

"Oh, my husband! My husband!"

If she had designed to say more, utterance failed, or was checked; for she hid her face on his bosom, and wept like a heart-broken child.

How sincere was Wilkinson's repentance for past errors in that solemn hour! and how fervent was the promise of future amendment!

"I were worse than an evil spirit, to lay grief upon that gentle heart, or to make of those loving eyes a fountain of tears!"

Such was the mental ejaculation of Wilkinson, and he meant all that he said.

"God bless you, dearest!" he murmured in her ear. - "God bless you, and take this shadow quickly from your heart! Believe me, Mary, that no act of mine will ever dim its bright surface again."

Mrs. Wilkinson slowly raised her pale, tear-moistened

face, and fixed, for a few moments, her eyes in those of her husband's. There was more of confidence and hope in them than pages of written language could express. Then her face was again hid on his bosom; while his arm clasped her slender form with a more earnest pressure.

CHAPTER VI

MORNING found little Ella, though much exhausted by the severe struggle through which she had passed, so far restored that her parents ceased to feel that anxiety with which for hours, as they hung over her, their hearts had been painfully oppressed.

It could not but be that a shadow would rest on the gentle face of Mrs. Wilkinson, as she met her husband at the breakfast table; for it was impossible to obliterate the memory of such a night of trial and alarm as the one through which she had just passed. And yet, with a strong effort, she strove to appear cheerful, and when she spoke to her husband, it was with a forced smile and a tone of tenderness that touched and subdued his feelings; for he well understood that, in a certain sense, she was merely acting.

But few words passed between them during the brief morning meal. As the hour was later than usual, Wilkinson found it necessary to hurry off to his place of business; so, rising before his wife left the table, he kissed her pale lips, and, without venturing to make a remark, left the room.

The door had scarcely closed upon him, ere a tear stole out from the sad eyes of Mrs. Wilkinson. A few moments she sat in statue-like stillness, then there was a quick glancing of her eye upwards, while the motion of her lips showed that she asked strength for herself, or protection for one whom she loved better than herself.

It was a regular custom with Wilkinson to stop at a drinking-house on his way to his store, and get a glass of brandy. This was an afternoon as well as a morning custom, which had been continued so long that it was now a habit. Yet he was not aware of this fact, and, if he had thought about the custom, would have regarded it as one easily abandoned. He had a glimpse of his error on the present occasion.

To do a thing by habit is to do it without reflection; and herein lies the dangerous power of habit; for, when we act from confirmed habit, it is without thought as to the good or evil to result from our action. Thus had Wilkinson been acting for months as regards his regular glass of brandy in the morning and afternoon, while passing from his dwelling to his store. Not until now was he in the least conscious that habit was gaining an undue power over him.

As the eyes of Wilkinson rested upon the form of a certain elegant coloured glass lamp standing in front of a well-known drinking-house, he was conscious of a desire for his accustomed draught of brandy and water; but, at the same instant, there came a remembrance of the painful occurrences of the evening previous, and he said to himself - "One such lesson ought to make me hate brandy, and every thing else that can rob me of a true regard for the happiness of Mary."

Yet, even as he said this, habit, disturbed in the stronghold of its power, aroused itself, and furnished

T. S. Arthur

him with an argument that instantly broke down his forming resolution. This argument was his loss of rest, the consequent debility arising therefrom, and the actual need of his system for something stimulating, in order to enable him to enter properly upon the business of the day.

So habit triumphed. Wilkinson, without even pausing at the door, entered the drinking-house and obtained his accustomed glass of brandy.

"I feel a hundred per cent. better," said he, as he emerged from the bar-room and took his way to his store. "That was just what my system wanted."

Yet, if he felt, for a little while, better as regarded his bodily sensations, the act did not leave him more comfortable in mind. His instinctive consciousness of having done wrong in yielding to the desire for brandy, troubled him.

"I shall have to break up this habit entirely," he remarked to himself during the morning, as his thought returned, again and again, to the subject. "I don't believe I'm in any particular danger; but, then, it troubles Mary; and I can't bear to see her troubled."

While he thus communed with himself, his friend Ellis dropped in.

I meant to have called earlier," said Ellis, "to ask about your sick child, but was prevented by a customer. She is better, I hope?"

"Oh, yes, much better, thank you."

"What was the matter?" inquired Ellis.

"She is teething, and was thrown into convulsions."

"Ah! yes. Well, I never was so startled in my life as by the appearance of Mrs. Wilkinson. And the child is better?"

"When I came away this morning, I left her sleeping calmly and sweetly; and, what is more, the points of two teeth had made their way through the red and swollen gums."

"All right, then. But how is Mary?"

"Not very well, of course. How could she be, after such a night of anxiety and alarm? The fact is, Harry, I was to blame for having left her alone during the evening, knowing, as I did, that Ella was not very well."

Ellis shrugged his shoulders, as he replied - "Not much excuse for you, I must admit. I only wish the attraction at my home was as strong as it is at yours: Parker's would not see me often. As for you, my old friend, if I speak what I think, I must say that your inclination to go out in the evening needs correcting. I spend most of my evenings from home, because home is made unpleasant; you leave your wife, because a love of conviviality and gay company entices you away. Such company I know to be dangerous, and especially so for you. There now, as a friend, I have talked out plainly. What do you think of it? Ain't I right?"

"I don't know," replied Wilkinson, musingly. "Perhaps you are. I have thought as much, sometimes, myself."

T. S. Arthur

"I know I'm right," said Ellis, positively. "So take a friend's advice, and never go out after sundown, except in company with your wife."

There was a change from gravity to mock seriousness in the voice of Ellis as he closed this sentence. Wilkinson compressed his lips and shook his head.

"Can't always be tied to my wife's apron-string. Oh, no! haven't come to that."

"With such a wife, and your temperament, it is the best place for you," said Ellis, laughing.

"May be it is; but, for all that, I like good company too well to spend all my time with her."

"Isn't she good company?"

"Oh, yes; but, then, variety is the very spice of life, you know."

"True enough. Well, we'll not quarrel about the matter. Come! let's go and take a drink; I'm as dry as a fish."

"I don't care if I do," was the instinctive reply of Wilkinson, who took up his hat as he spoke.

The two men left the store, and were, a little while after, taking a lunch at a public house, and chatting over their brandy and water.

At the usual dinner hour, Wilkinson returned home. He did not fully understand the expression of his wife's face, as she looked at him on his entrance: it was a look of anxious inquiry. She sat with Ella upon her lap:

the child was sleeping.

"How is our little pet?" he asked, as he bent over, first kissing his wife, and then touching his lips lightly to the babe's forehead.

"She's been in a heavy sleep for most of the time since morning," replied Mrs. Wilkinson, turning her face aside, so that her husband could not see its changed expression.

Mr. Wilkinson's habitual use of brandy had long been a source of trouble to his wife. In reviewing the painful incidents of the previous evening, a hope had sprung up in her heart that the effect would be to awaken his mind to a sense of his danger, cause him to reflect, and lead to a change of habit. Alas! how like a fairy frost-work fabric melted this hope away, as the strong breath of her husband fell upon her face. She turned away and sighed - sighed in her spirit, but not audibly; for, even in her pain and disappointment, active love prompted to concealment, lest the shadow that came over her should repel the one she so earnestly sought to win from his path of danger.

Ah, who can tell the effort it cost that true-hearted wife to call up the smile with which, scarcely a moment afterwards, she looked into her husband's face!

"It is no worse, if no better," was her sustaining thought; and she leaned upon it, fragile reed as it was.

T. S. Arthur

CHAPTER VII

"COME home early, dear," said Mrs. Wilkinson, resting her hand upon her husband, and looking into his face with a loving smile. "The time seems so long when you are away!"

"Does it?" returned Wilkinson, and he kissed his wife. Yet, did not the tenderness of tone with which he spoke, nor the act of love which accompanied it, hide from the quick perception of Mary the fact that her husband's thoughts were elsewhere.

"Oh, yes," she replied. "I count the hours when you are absent. You'll be home early to tea?"

"Certainly I will. There now, let your heart be at rest."

And Wilkinson retired. This was after dinner, on the day that succeeded the opening of our story.

As in the morning, he found it the most natural thing in the world to call in at a certain drinking house and get his accustomed glass of brandy. As he entered the door of the bar-room, a man named Carlton stepped forward to meet him, with extended hand. He was an old acquaintance, with whom Wilkinson had often passed an agreeable hour, - one of your bar-room loungers, known as good fellows, who, while they exhibit no apparent means of support, generally have money to spend, and plenty of time on their hands.

"Glad to see you, Wilkinson; 'pon my soul! Where have you kept yourself for this month of Sundays?"

Such was the familiar greeting of Carlton.

"And it does one's eyes good to look upon your pleasant face," returned Wilkinson, as he grasped the other's hand. "Where have you kept yourself?"

"Oh, I'm always on hand," said Carlton, gayly. "It's you who are shut up, and hid away from the pure air and bright sunshine in a gloomy store, delving like a mole in the dark. The fact is, old fellow! you are killing yourself. Turning gray, as I live!"

And he touched, with his fingers, the locks of Wilkinson, in which a few gray lines were visible.

"Bad! bad!" he went on, shaking his head. "And you are growing as thin as a lath. When did you ride out?"

"Oh, not for two months past. I've been too closely occupied with business."

"Business!" there was a slight air of contempt in Carlton's voice and manner. "I hate to hear this everlasting cant, if I must so call it, about business; as if there were nothing else in the world to think or care about. Men bury themselves between four brick walls, and toil from morning until night, like prison-slaves; and if you talk to them about an hour's recreation for body and mind, all you can get out of them is - 'Business! business!' Pah! I'm out of all patience with

T. S. Arthur

it. Life was made for enjoyment as well as toil. But come, what'll you drink? I've preached to you until I'm as dry as a chip."

The two men stepped to the bar and drank. As they turned away, Carlton drew his arm within that of Wilkinson, saying, as he did so -

"As it is an age since I saw you, I must prolong the pleasure of this meeting. Your work is done for the day, of course."

"No, I can't just say that it is."

"Well, I can then. If you've been immuring yourself, as you have on your own confession, for some two months, or more, an afternoon with good company is indispensable. So, consider this a holiday, and think no more of bags, boxes, cash-book, or ledger. I bought a splendid trotter yesterday, and am going to try his speed. You are a first-rate judge of horse-flesh, and I want your opinion. So, consider yourself engaged for a flying trip to Mount Airy."

"You are a tempter," said Wilkinson, laughing.

"Oh, no. A friend, who will give health to your veins, and life to your spirit."

"Let me see," said Wilkinson, now turning his thoughts upon his business - "if there isn't something special that requires my attention. Yes," he added, after thinking for a few moments - "a customer promised to be in after dinner. He is from the country, and bought a good bill last season. You will have to excuse me, Carlton.

I'll go with you to-morrow."

"Indeed, and I shall do no such thing," was promptly answered. "Let your customers call in the morning - always the best time for business. Men don't buy in the afternoon."

"My experience says differently."

"A fig for your experience! No, no, my good friend. You're booked for a ride with me this very afternoon; so let your business and customers take care of themselves. Health is better than dollars; and length of days than great possessions. There's wisdom in miniature for you. Wouldn't I make a capital preacher, ha?"

"But Carlton" -

"But me no buts, my hearty!" and Carlton slapped Wilkinson on the shoulder as he spoke, in a familiar manner. "You're my prisoner for the rest of the day. Do you understand that?"

"You've bought a fast trotter, have you?" said Wilkinson, after a brief but hurried self-communion, the end of which was a determination to take the afternoon for pleasure, and let his customer call in the morning.

"I have; and the prettiest animal your eyes ever looked upon."

"Fleet as an arrow?"

"Ay; as the very wind. But you shall have a taste of his

quality. So come along. Time passes."

The two men left the tavern, and went to the stable where Carlton's new horse was kept. The animal was soon in harness.

Four hours afterwards, the last rays of the setting sun came through the windows of a room, in which were seated, at a table, Carlton and Wilkinson. Liquor and glasses were on the table, and cards in the hands of the men. Wilkinson appeared excited, but Carlton was calm and self-possessed. The former had been drinking freely; but the latter exhibited not the smallest sign of inebriation. A single five-dollar bill lay beside Wilkinson; a dozen bills and two gold coins were beside the other. They were playing for the last stake. Nervously did Wilkinson lay card after card upon the table, while, with the most perfect coolness, his adversary played his hand, a certainty of winning apparent in every motion. And he did win.

"Curse my luck!" exclaimed Wilkinson, grinding his teeth together, as the last five-dollar bill he had with him passed into the hands of his very particular friend.

There was more than "luck" against him, if he had but known it.

"The fortune of war," smilingly replied the winner. "The race is not always to the swift, nor the battle to the strong, you know. You played well - very well; never better within my knowledge. But, as you say, luck was against you. And, by the way, what a curious and uncertain thing this luck is! I've seen men lose at every turn of the card, until they had parted with thousands; and then, on a borrowed dollar, perhaps, start again, and not only get every thing back, but break their antagonists. This is an every-day occurrence, in fact."

Wilkinson had risen from the table, and was pacing the room in a fretful, impatient manner. Suddenly he stopped. A light flashed over his face. Then, sitting down, he snatched up a pen, and writing on a slip of paper - "Due Andrew Carlton $20," signed it with his name.

Carlton saw every letter and word as they left the pen, and ere the last flourish was made to the signature, had selected four five-dollar bills from the pile beside him. Simultaneously with the motion of Wilkinson's hand, in pushing to him this memorandum of debt, was the motion of his hand in furnishing the sum required.

"Not the man to be frightened at a little adverse fortune, I see," remarked the cunning tempter. "Well, I do like a man who never can acknowledge himself beaten. The timid and easily discouraged are soon left far behind in the world's race - and they deserve to be."

Wilkinson did not reply. Another deal was made, and again the two men bent over the table in their unequal contest.

In less than half an hour, the money obtained from Carlton had gone back to him.

By this time twilight had fallen.

"Nearly eight o'clock, as I live!" muttered Wilkinson. He had drawn forth his watch. "I had no idea of this. And we are ten miles from the city!"

A thought of his anxiously waiting wife flitted across his mind. He remembered her last pleading injunction for him to come home early, and the promise he had given. Alas! like so many more of his promises to her, made to be broken.

"Shall we return now; or order supper here?" said Carlton, in his bland way.

"I must go back immediately," replied Wilkinson. "It is an hour later than I supposed. I was to have been home early this evening."

"It is too late now to join your family at tea. They have given you out before this. So, I think we'd better order supper here. The moon is full, and it will be almost as clear as daylight; and much pleasanter riding, for the dew will keep down the dust. What say you?"

The end was, Wilkinson yielded.

"Not down in the mouth, because of this little run of ill-luck?" said Carlton, in a bantering way, as he saw a cloud settling over the face of his victim.

Lights had been brought in, and the two men still remained seated by the table at which they had been playing, awaiting the preparation of supper.

I'm never down in the mouth," replied Wilkinson, forcing a smile to his countenance. "Better luck next time, has always been my motto."

"And it will carry you safely through the world. Try another glass of brandy."

"No - I've taken enough already."

"It isn't every man who knows when he has enough," returned the other. "I've often wished that I knew exactly the right guage."

And, as Carlton spoke, he poured some brandy into a glass, and, adding a little water, affected to take a deep draught thereof; but, though the glass was held long to his mouth, only a small portion of the contents passed his lips. In replacing the tumbler on the table, he managed to give it a position behind the water-pitcher where the eye of Wilkinson could not rest upon it. He need hardly have taken this trouble, for his companion was too much absorbed in his own thoughts to notice a matter like this.

"They're a long time in getting supper," remarked Carlton, in a well-affected tone of impatience. "What is the time now?"

Wilkinson drew forth his watch, and, after glancing upon the face, replied -

"Ten minutes after eight."

"We shall have it pretty soon now, I suppose. They don't understand the double quick time movement out here."

As Carlton said this, his eyes rested, with more than a mere passing interest, on the gold lever that Wilkinson, instead of returning to his pocket, retained in one hand, while with the other he toyed with the key and chain in a half-abstracted manner.

T. S. Arthur

For the space of nearly a minute, neither of the men spoke, but the thought of each was at the same point.

"That's a beautiful watch," at length Carlton ventured to say. There was a well disguised indifference in his tones.

"It ought to be," was the reply of Wilkinson.

"What did it cost you?"

"One hundred and forty dollars."

"Is it a good time-keeper?"

"First-rate. It hasn't varied a minute in six months."

"Just such a watch as I would like to own. I've had terrible bad luck with watches."

This was a kind of feeler.

No reply was made by Wilkinson, although an offer to sell trembled on his tongue. He still kept the watch in his hand, and toyed with the key and chain, as before, in an absent manner.

"Could you be tempted to sell?" finally asked Carlton.

"I don't know. Perhaps I might," - said Wilkinson. He drew his breath deeply as he spoke.

"Or, perhaps you would trade?" and Carlton now produced his gold lever. "Mine is a very good watch, though not so valuable as yours. It keeps fair time, however. I paid a hundred dollars for it three or four years ago."

A mutual examination of watches took place.

"Well - what do you say to a trade?"

The servant appeared at this juncture, and announced supper. The two watches were returned to their respective places of deposit, and the two men proceeded to the dining-room. Here the traffic, just begun, was renewed and completed. The watches were exchanged, and Wilkinson received sixty dollars "boot."

"Shall I order the horse brought out?" asked Carlton, as they arose, about half an hour afterwards, from the supper-table.

"Yes; if you please."

This was not said with much promptness of tone; a fact instantly noted by the ear of Carlton.

"Well, I'm ready. Come - let's have a drink before we go!"

The two men stepped to the bar and drank. Then they lingered, each with a lighted cigar, and finally withdrew - to proceed to the city? No. To return to their room up-stairs, and renew their unequal contest. The sixty dollars which Wilkinson had received were staked, and soon passed over to his adversary. Rendered, now, desperate by his losses and the brandy which inflamed his brain, he borrowed, once more, on his due-bill - this time to the amount of several hundred dollars. His ill-success continued.

T. S. Arthur

It was nearly eleven o'clock, when Wilkinson started up from the table, exclaiming, as he threw the cards upon the floor -

"Fool! fool! fool! One step more, and I am ruined. Carlton!" And he fixed his eyes almost fiercely upon his companion.

"Carlton! I thought you my friend, but find, when it is almost too late to profit by the discovery, that you are a tempter. Ay! and worse than a tempter. Pure air and the bright sunshine! Is this your health for mind and body? Oh! weak, weak, unstable one that I am! Poor Mary!" This was said in a low, mournful, and scarcely audible voice. "Thus has my promise to you vanished into thin air!"

As Wilkinson said this, he turned away and left the room. Carlton was in no hurry to follow. When, at length, he came down, and made inquiry for the one he had dealt by so treacherously, the man, who was shutting the windows of the bar-room, and about locking up for the night, replied that he had not seen him.

"Not seen him?" he asked, in a tone of surprise.

"No, sir. He didn't come in here."

The hostler was aroused from his sleeping position on a bench in the corner, and directed by Carlton to bring out his buggy. During the time he was away, the latter made a hurried search in and around the house. Not finding the object thereof, he muttered, in an under tone, a few wicked oaths; then, jumping into his vehicle, he put whip to his horse, and dashed off towards the city. He had Wilkinson's due-bills in his pocket for various sums, amounting, in all, to nearly two thousand dollars!

T. S. Arthur

CHAPTER VIII

ALMOST motionless, with her sleeping babe upon her lap, sat Mrs. Wilkinson for nearly half an hour after her husband left the house. She saw nothing that was around her - heard nothing - felt nothing. Not even the breathings of her sleeping infant reached her ear; nor was she conscious of the pressure of its body against her own. Fixed in a dreamy, inward gaze were her eyes; and her soul withdrew itself from the portal at which, a little while before, it hearkened into the world of nature. At last there came a motion of the eyelids - a quivering motion - then they closed, slowly, over the blue orbs beneath; and soon after a tear trembled out to the light from behind the barriers that sought to retain them. A deep, fluttering sigh succeeded to this sign of feeling. Then her lips parted, and she spoke audibly to herself.

"Oh, that I knew how to win him back from the path of danger! He does not love his home; and yet how have I striven to make it attractive! How much have I denied myself! and how much yielded to and thought of him! He is always kind to me; and he - yes - I know he loves me; but - ah!"

The low voice trembled back sighing into silence. Still, for a long time, the unhappy wife sat almost as motionless as if in sleep. Then, as some thought grew active towards a purpose in her mind, she arose, and laying Ella on the bed, began busying herself in some household duties.

The afternoon passed slowly away, yet not for a moment was the thought of her husband absent from the mind of Mrs. Wilkinson.

"What ought I to do? How shall I make his home sufficiently attractive?"

This was her over and over again repeated question; and her thoughts bent themselves eagerly for some answer upon which her heart might rest with even a small degree of hope.

The prolonged, intense anxiety and alarm of the previous night, added to bodily fatigue and loss of rest, were not without their effect upon Mrs. Wilkinson. Early in the day she suffered from lassitude and a sense of exhaustion; and, after dinner, a slight head-ache was added; this increased hourly, and by four o'clock was almost blinding in its violence. Still, she tried to forget herself, and what she suffered in thinking about and devising some means of saving her husband from the dangers that lay hidden from his own view about his footsteps.

"If I could only add some new attraction to his home!" she murmured to herself, over and over again.

Sometimes she would hold her temples with both her hands, in the vain effort to still, by pressure, the throbbing arteries within, while she continued to think of her husband.

T. S. Arthur

As tea-time drew near, Mrs. Wilkinson left Ella in the care of a domestic, and went into the kitchen to prepare some delicacy for the evening meal of which she knew her husband was fond; this engaged her for half an hour, and the effort increased the pain in her aching head.

The usual time at which Mr. Wilkinson came home arrived, and his wife, who had returned to her chamber, sat with her babe on her bosom, listening for the well-known welcome sound of her husband's footsteps in the passage below. Time glided by, yet she waited and listened in vain; and to the pleasant thoughts of the influence her love was to throw around him on that very evening, to keep him at home, began to succeed a fear, which made her heart faint, that he would not come home at all; or, at least, not until a late hour.

The sun went down, and stealthily the sober twilight began to fall, bringing with it shadows and forebodings for the heart of the anxious wife.

How vainly she waited and watched! The twilight was lost in darkness, and yet her eagerly listening ear failed to note the well-known sound of her husband's footfall on the pavement, as she stood, listening at the open window.

"Oh! what can keep him so long away!"

How often did these words come sighing from her lips, yet there was no answer. Alas! how to the very winds were flung the pleasant hopes she had cherished - cherished with a sense of fear and trembling - during the afternoon.

Night closed in, and the time wore on steadily, minute by minute, and hour by hour, until the poor wife was almost wild with suspense and anxiety. The dainties she had so thoughtfully and lovingly prepared for her husband remained untasted, and had now become cold and unpalatable - were, in fact, forgotten. Food she had not, herself, tasted. Once or twice a servant had come to know if she would have tea served; but she merely answered - "Not until Mr. Wilkinson returns."

Nine - ten - eleven o'clock; still Mrs. Wilkinson was alone. Sometimes she moved restlessly about her chamber; or wandered, like a perturbed spirit, from room to room; and, sometimes in mere exhaustion, would drop into a chair or sink across the bed, and sit or lie as motionless as if in a profound sleep.

Ah! could her husband have looked in upon her, but for a few moments; could he have seen the anguish of her pale face; the fixed and dreamy expression of her tearful eyes; the grieving arch of the lips he loved - could he have seen and comprehended all she suffered and all she feared, it must have won him back from his selfish folly. And how many wives have suffered all this, and more! How many still suffer! Errant husband, pause, look upon the picture we have presented, and think of the many, many heart-aches you have given the tender, long-suffering, loving one who clings to you yet so closely, and who, for your sake, would even lay down, if needful, her very life.

Happily for Mrs. Wilkinson, her child lay in a sound sleep; for, with the appearance of the edges of two teeth through her red and swollen gums, the feverish excitement of her system yielded to a healthy reaction.

T. S. Arthur

Twelve o'clock was rung out clearly upon the hushed air of midnight; and yet the poor wife was alone. One o'clock found her in a state of agonized alarm, standing at the open street-door, and hearkening, eagerly, first in one direction and then in another; yet all in vain - for the absent one came not.

It was nearly two o'clock, and Mrs. Wilkinson, in the impotence of her prolonged and intense anxiety and fear, had thrown herself, with a groan, across her bed, when a sound in the street caught her ear. Instantly she started up, while a thrill ran through every nerve. Feet were on the door-steps; a key was in the lock - a moment more, and the door opened and shut, and a familiar tread that made her heart leap echoed along the passage. Her first impulse was to fly to meet the comer, but a hand seemed to hold her back; and so, half reclining, she awaited, with her heart beating violently, the appearance of him whose strange absence had cost her so many hours of bitter anguish. A moment or two more, and then an exclamation of surprise and almost terror, fell from her lips. And well might she be startled at the appearance of her husband.

Pale, haggard, covered with dust, and with large drops of perspiration on his face, Wilkinson stood before his wife. With a grieving look he gazed upon her for some moments, but did not speak.

"My husband!" exclaimed Mrs. Wilkinson as soon as she could recover herself; and, as she uttered the words, she threw her arms around him, and buried her weeping face on his bosom.

But Wilkinson tried to disengage her arms, saying, as he did so -

"Not this! - not this, Mary! I am unworthy of even your feeblest regard. Speak to me coldly, harshly, angrily, if you will. That I deserve - but nothing of kindness, nothing of love. Oh, that I were dead!"

"My husband! my husband! you are dearer to me than life!" was whispered in reply, as Mary clung to him more closely.

Such evidences of love melted the strong man's heart. He tried to brace himself up against what, in his pride, he felt to be a weakness, but failed, and leaning his face downward until it rested upon the head of his wife, sobbed aloud.

CHAPTER IX

WILKINSON, on leaving the presence of the man who, under the guise of friendship, had so basely led him astray, and robbed him - it was robbery, in fact, for Carlton had not only enticed his victim to drink until his mind was confused, but had played against him with trick and false dealing - passed, not by the bar-room of the hotel, but through one of the passages, into the open air, and with hurried steps, and mind all in a whirl of excitement, started on foot for home. He was not in a state to consider exactly what he was doing - he did not reflect that he was at least ten miles from the city, and that it would take him hours to walk that distance. His predominant feeling was a desire to escape from the presence of the man who had so basely betrayed and almost ruined him.

It was a calm, clear, summer night; and the full moon, which had reached the zenith, shone with an unusual radiance. Not a leaf moved on the forest trees, for even the zephyrs were asleep. All was stillness and tranquil beauty.

Yet nature did not mirror herself on the feelings of Wilkinson, for their surface was in wild commotion. The unhappy man was conscious only of the folly he had committed and the wrong he had sustained; and thought only of his culpable weakness in having been drawn, by a specious villain, to the very verge of ruin.

Onward he strode, toward the city, with rapid pace, and soon his thoughts began to go forward towards his home.

"Poor Mary!" he sighed, as the image of his wife, when she said to him - "I count the hours when you are away," arose before his eyes. Then, as the image grew more and more distinct, his hands were clenched tightly, and he murmured through his shut teeth -

"Wretch! cruel wretch, that I am! I shall break her heart! Oh, why did I not resist this temptation? Why was I so thoughtless of the best, the truest, the most loving friend I ever knew or ever can know - my Mary!"

Rapid as his steps had been from the first, the thought of his wife caused Wilkinson to increase his pace, and he moved along, the only passenger at that hour upon the road, at almost a running speed. Soon the perspiration was gushing freely from every pore, and this, in a short time, relieved the still confused pressure on the brain of the alcohol which had been taken so freely into his system. Thoroughly sobered was he, ere he had passed over half the distance; and the clearer his mind became, the more troubled grew his feelings.

"What," he repeated to himself, over and over, "what if our dear Ella should be in convulsions again?"

So great was the anguish of the unhappy man, that he was all unconscious of bodily fatigue. He was nearly half way to the city when overtaken by Carlton. The latter called to him three or four times, and invited him to get up and ride; but Wilkinson strode on, without so much as uttering a word in reply, or seeming to hear what was said to him. So Carlton, finding that his proffer was disregarded, dashed ahead and was soon out of sight.

At what hour Wilkinson reached his home, and how he was received, has already been seen.

Too heavy a pressure lay on the mind of the unhappy man, as he met his wife at the breakfast table on the next morning, for him even to make an effort at external cheerfulness. There was not only the remembrance of his broken promise, and the anguish she must have suffered in consequence of his absence for half the night - how visible, alas! was the effect written on her pale face, and eyes still red and swollen from excessive tears - but the remembrance, also, that he had permitted himself, while under the influence of drink, to lose some two thousand dollars at the gaming table! What would he not endure to keep that blasting fact from the knowledge of his single-hearted, upright companion? He a gambler! How sick at heart the thought made him feel, when that thought came into the presence of his wife!

Few words passed between Mr. and Mrs. Wilkinson, but the manner of each was subdued, gentle, and even affectionate. They parted, after the morning meal, in silence; Wilkinson to repair to his place of business, his wife to busy herself in household duties, and await with trembling anxiety the return of her husband at the regular dinner hour.

This time, Wilkinson did not, as usual, drop in at a certain drinking-house that was in his way, but kept on direct to his store. The reason of this omission of his habitual glass of brandy was not, we are compelled to say, from a purpose in his mind to abandon the dangerous practice, but to avoid encountering the man Carlton, who might happen to be there. But he was not to keep clear of him in this way. Oh, no. Carlton held his due-bills for "debts of honour," calling for various sums, amounting in all, as we have before said, to about two thousand dollars, and he was not a person at all likely to forget this fact. Of this Wilkinson was made sensible, about an hour after appearing at his store. He was at his desk musing over certain results figured out on a sheet of paper that lay before him, and which had reference to payments to be made during the next three or four weeks, when he heard his name mentioned, and, turning, saw a stranger addressing one of his clerks, who had just pointed to where he was sitting. The man, with his unpleasant eyes fixed upon Wilkinson, came, with firm yet deliberate steps, back to his desk.

"Mr. Wilkinson, I believe?" said he.

"That is my name." Wilkinson tried to feel self-possessed and indifferent. But that was impossible, for he had an instinctive knowledge of the purport of the visit.

The man thrust his hand into a deep inside pocket, and abstracted therefrom a huge pocket-book. He did not search long in the compartments of this for what he wanted, but drew directly therefrom sundry small, variously shaped pieces of paper, much blotted and scrawled over in a hurried hand. Each of these bore the signature of Wilkinson, and words declaring himself indebted in a certain sum to Andrew Carlton.

T. S. Arthur

"I am desired to collect these," said the man coldly.

Much as Wilkinson had thought, in anticipation of this particular crisis, he was yet undecided as to what he should do. He had been made the victim of a specious scoundrel - a wolf who had come to him in sheep's clothing. Running back his thoughts, as distinctly as it was possible for him to do, to the occurrences of the previous night, he remembered much that fully satisfied him that Carlton had played against him most unfairly; he not only induced him to drink until his mind was confused, but had taken advantage of this confused state, to cheat in the grossest manner. Some moments passed ere he replied to the application; then he said -

"I'm not prepared to do any thing with this matter just now."

"My directions are to collect these bills," was the simple reply, made in a tone that expressed even more than the words.

"You may find that more difficult than you imagine," replied Wilkinson, with some impatience.

"No - no - we never have much difficulty in collecting debts of this kind." There was a meaning emphasis on the last two words, which Wilkinson understood but too well. Still he made answer,

"You may find it a little harder in the present case than you imagine. I never received value for these tokens of indebtedness."

"You must have been a precious fool to have given

them then," was promptly returned, with a curling lip, and in a tone of contempt. "They represent, I presume, debts of honour?"

"There was precious little honour in the transaction," said Wilkinson, who, stung by the manner and words of the collector, lost his self-possessions. "If ever a man was cheated, I was."

"Say that to Mr. Carlton himself; it is out of place with me. As I remarked a little while ago, my business is to collect the sums called for by these due-bills. Are you prepared to settle them?"

"No," was the decisive answer.

"Perhaps," said the collector, who had his part to play, and who, understanding it thoroughly, showed no inclination to go off in a huff; "you do not clearly understand your position, nor the consequences likely to follow the answer just given; that is, if you adhere to your determination not to settle these due-bills."

"You'll make the effort to collect by law, I presume?"

"Of course we will."

"And get nothing. The law will not recognise a debt of this kind."

"How is the law to come at the nature of the debt?"

"I will" - Wilkinson stopped suddenly.

"Will you?" quickly chimed in the collector. "Then you are a bolder, or rather, more reckless man than I took you for. Your family, friends, creditors, and mercantile associates will be edified, no doubt, when it comes to light on the trial, under your own statement, that you have been losing large sums of money at the gaming table - over two thousand dollars in a single night."

A strong exclamation came from the lips of Wilkinson, who saw the trap into which he had fallen, and from which there was, evidently, no safe mode of escape.

"It is impossible for me to pay two thousand dollars now," said he, after a long, agitated silence, during which he saw, more clearly than before, the unhappy position in which he was placed. "It will be ruin anyhow; and if loss of credit and character are to come, it might as well come with the most in hand I can retain."

"You are the best judge of that," said the collector, coldly, turning partly away as he spoke.

"Tell Carlton that I would like to see him."

"He left the city this morning," replied the collector.

"Left the city?"

"Yes, sir; and you will perceive that all of these due-bills have been endorsed to me, and are, consequently, my property, for which I have paid a valuable consideration. They are, therefore, legal claims against you in the fullest sense, and I am not the man to waive my rights, or to be thwarted in my purposes. Are you prepared to settle?"

"Not to-day, at least."

"I am not disposed to be too hard with you," said the man, slightly softening in his tone; "and will say at a word what I will do, and all I will do. You can take up five hundred of these bills to-day, five hundred in one week, and the balance in equal sums at two and three weeks. I yield this much; but, understand me, it is all I yield, and you need not ask for any further consideration.

"Well, sir, what do you say?" Full five minutes after the collector had given his ultimatum, he thus broke in upon the perplexed and undecided silence of the unhappy victim of his own weakness and folly. "Am I to receive five hundred dollars now, or am I not?"

"Call in an hour, and I will be prepared to give an answer," said Wilkinson.

"Very well. I'll be here in one hour to a minute," and the man consulted his watch.

And to a minute was he there.

"Well, sir, have you decided this matter?" said he, on confronting Wilkinson an hour later. He spoke with the air of one who felt indifferent as to which way the decision had been made. Without replying, Wilkinson took from under a paper weight on his desk a check for five hundred dollars, and presented it to the collector.

"All right," was the satisfied remark of the latter as he read the face of the check; and, immediately producing his large pocket-book, drew forth Wilkinson's due-bills, and selecting one for three hundred and one for two hundred dollars, placed them in his hands.

"On this day one week I will be here again," said the man, impressively, and, turning away, left the store.

The moment he was out of sight, Wilkinson tore the due-bills he had cancelled into a score of pieces, and, as he scattered them on the floor, said to himself - "Perish, sad evidences of my miserable folly! The lesson would be salutary, were it not received at too heavy a cost. Can I recover from this? Alas! I fear not. Fifteen hundred more to be abstracted from my business, and in three weeks! How can it possibly be done?"

To a certain extent, the lesson was salutary. During the next three weeks, Wilkinson, who felt a nervous reluctance to enter a drinking-house lest he should meet Carlton, kept away from such places, and therefore drank but little during the time; nor did he once go out in the evening, except in company with his wife, who was studious, all the time, in the science of making home happy. But it was impossible for her to chase away the shadow that rested upon her husband's brow.

Promptly, on a certain day in each week of that period, came the man who held the due-bills given to Carlton, leaving Wilkinson five hundred dollars poorer with each visitation - poorer, unhappier, and more discouraged in regard to his business, which was scarcely stanch enough to bear the sudden withdrawal of so much money.

Under such circumstances it was impossible for Wilkinson to appear otherwise than troubled. To divine the cause of this trouble soon became the central purpose in the mind of his wife. To all her questions on the subject, he gave evasive answers; still she gathered enough to satisfy her that every thing was not right in regard to his business. Assuming this to be the case, she began to think over the ways and means of reducing their range of expenses, which were in the neighbourhood of fifteen hundred dollars per annum. The result will appear.

T. S. Arthur

CHAPTER X

THE morning of the day came on which Wilkinson had to make his last payment on account of the due-bills given to Carlton. He had nothing in bank, and there were few borrowing resources not already used to the utmost limit. At ten o'clock he went out to see what could be done in the way of effecting further temporary loans among business friends. His success was not very great, for at twelve o'clock he returned with only two hundred dollars. Carlton's agent had called twice during the time, and came in a few minutes afterwards.

"You're too soon for me," said Wilkinson, with not a very cheerful or welcome expression of countenance.

"It's past twelve," returned the man.

"All the same if it were past three. I haven't the money."

The collector's brow lowered heavily.

"How soon will you have it?"

"Can't tell," replied Wilkinson, fretfully.

"That kind of answer don't just suit me," said the man,

with some appearance of anger. "I've been remarkable easy with you, and now" -

"Easy!" sharply ejaculated Wilkinson. "Yes; as the angler who plays his trout. You've already received fifteen hundred dollars of the sum out of which I was swindled, and with that I should think both you and your principal might be content. Go back to him, and say that he is about placing on the camel's back the pound that may break it."

"I have before told you," was replied, "that Mr. Carlton has no longer any control in this matter. It is I who hold your obligations; they have been endorsed to me, and for a valuable consideration; and be assured that I shall exact the whole bond."

"If," said Wilkinson, after some moments' reflection, and speaking in a changed voice and with much deliberation, "if you will take my note of hand for the amount of your due-bills, at six months from to-day, I will give it; if not" -

"Preposterous!" returned the man, interrupting him.

"If not," continued Wilkinson, "you can fall back upon the law. It has its delays and chances; and I am more than half inclined to the belief that I was a fool not to have left this matter for a legal decision in the beginning. I should have gained time at least."

"If you are so anxious to get into court, you can be gratified," was answered.

"Very well; seek your redress in law," said Wilkinson, angrily. "Occasionally, gamblers and pickpockets get to the end of their rope; and, perhaps, it may turn out so in this instance. My only regret now is, that I didn't let the matter go to court in the beginning."

The man turned off hastily, but paused ere he reached the door, stood musing for a while, and then came slowly back.

"Give me your note at sixty days," said he.

"No, sir," was the firm reply of Wilkinson. "I offered my note at six months. For not a day less will I give it; and I don't care three coppers whether you take it or no. I had about as lief test the matter in a court of justice as not."

The man again made a feint to retire, but again returned.

"Say three months, then."

"It is useless to chaffer with me, sir." Wilkinson spoke sternly. "I have said what I will do, and I will do nothing else. Even that offer I shall withdraw if not accepted now."

The man seemed thrown quite aback by the prompt and decisive manner of Wilkinson, and, after some hesitation and grumbling, finally consented to yield up the balance of the due-bills for a note payable in six months.

"Saved as by fire!" Such was the mental ejaculation of Wilkinson, as the collector left the store. "I stagger already under the extra weight of fifteen hundred dollars. Five hundred added now would come nigh to crushing me. Ah! how dearly have I paid for my folly!"

While he still sat musing at his desk, his friend Ellis came in, looking quite sober.

"I know you've been pretty hard run for the last week or ten days," said he, "but can't you strain a point and help me a little? I've been running about all the morning, and am still two hundred dollars short of the amount to be paid in bank to-day."

"Fortunately," replied Wilkinson, "I have just the sum you need."

"How long can you spare it?"

"Until day after to-morrow."

"You shall have it then, without fail."

The money was counted out and handed to Ellis, who, as he received it, said in a desponding voice -

"Unless a man is so fortunate as to be born with a silver spoon in his mouth, he finds nothing but up-hill work in this troublesome world. I declare! I'm almost discouraged. I can feel myself going behindhand, instead of advancing."

"Don't say that. You're only in a desponding mood," replied Wilkinson, repressing his own gloomy feelings, and trying to speak encouragingly.

"I wish it were only imagination. It is now nearly ten years since I was married, and though my business, at the time, was good, and paying a fair profit on the light capital invested, it has, instead of getting more prosperous, become, little and by little, embarrassed, until now - I speak this confidently, and to one whom I know to be a friend - were every thing closed up, I doubt if I should be worth five hundred dollars."

"Not so bad as that. You are only in a gloomy state of mind."

"I wish it were only nervous despondency, my friend. But it is not so. All the while I am conscious of a retrograde instead of an advance movement."

"There must be a cause for this," said Wilkinson.

"Of course. There is no effect without a cause."

"Do you know what it is?"

"Yes."

"A knowledge of our disease is said to be half the cure."

"It has not proved so in my case."

"What is the difficulty?"

"My expenses are too high."

"Your store expenses?"

"No, my family expenses."

"Then you ought to reduce them."

"That is easily said; but, in my case, not so easily done. I cannot make my wife comprehend the necessity of retrenchment."

"If you were to explain the whole matter to her, calmly and clearly, I am certain you would not find her unreasonable. Her stake in this matter is equal to yours."

"Oh, dear! Haven't I tried, over and over again?"

"If Cara will not hear reason, and join with you in prudent reforms, then it is your duty to make them yourself. What are your annual expenses?"

"I am ashamed to say."

"Fifteen hundred dollars?"

"They have never fallen below that since we were married, and, for the last three years, have reached the sum of two thousand dollars. This year they will even exceed that."

Wilkinson shook his head.

"Too much! too much!"

"I know it is. A man in my circumstances has no right to expend even half that sum. Why, five hundred dollars a year less in our expenses since we were married would have left me a capital of five thousand dollars in my business."

"And placed you now on the sure road to fortune."

"Undoubtedly."

"Take my advice, and give to Cara a full statement of your affairs. Do it at once - this very day. It has been put off too long already. Let there be no reserve - no holding back - no concealment. Do it calmly, mildly, yet earnestly, and my word for it, she will join you, heart and hand, in any measure of reform and safety that you may propose. She were less than a woman, a wife, and a mother, not to do so. You wrong her by doubt."

"Perhaps I do," said Ellis in reply. "Perhaps I have never managed her rightly. I know that I am quick to get out of patience with her, if she oppose my wishes too strongly. But I will try and overcome this. There is too much at stake just now."

The two men parted. Henry Ellis pondered all day over the present state of his affairs, and the absolute necessity there was for a reduction of his expenses. The house in which he lived cost four hundred and fifty dollars a year. Two hundred dollars could easily be saved, he thought, by taking a smaller house, where, if they were only willing to think so, they might be just as comfortable as they now were. Beyond this reduction in rent, Ellis did not see clearly how to proceed. The rest would have mainly to depend upon his wife, who had almost the entire charge of the home department, including the expenditures made on account thereof.

The earnestness with which Ellis pondered these things lifted his thoughts so much above the sensual plane where they too often rested, that he felt not the desire for stimulating drink returning at certain hours, but passed through the whole of the afternoon without either thinking of or tasting his usual glass of brandy and water. On coming home to his family in the evening, his mind was as clear as a bell. This, unhappily, was not always the case.

And now for the task of making Cara comprehend the real state of his affairs; and to produce in her a cheerful, loving, earnest co-operation in the work of salutary reform. But how to begin? What first to say? How to disarm her opposition in the outset? These were the questions over which Ellis pondered. And the difficulty loomed up larger and larger the nearer he approached it. He felt too serious; and was conscious of this.

Unhappily, Cara's brow was somewhat clouded. Ellis approached her with attempts at cheerful conversation; but she was not in the mood to feel interested in any of the topics he introduced. The tea hour passed with little of favourable promise. The toast was badly made, and the chocolate not half boiled. Mrs. Ellis was annoyed, and scolded the cook, in the presence of her husband, soundly; thus depriving him of the little appetite with which he had come to the table. Gradually the unhappy man felt his patience and forbearance leaving him; and more than once he said to himself -

"It will be worse than useless to talk to her. She will throw back my words upon me, in the beginning, as she has so often done before."

Tea over, Mr. and Mrs. Ellis returned with their children to the sitting-room. The former felt an almost irrepressible desire for the cigar, which habit had rendered so nearly indispensable; but he denied himself the indulgence, lest Cara should make it the occasion of some annoying remark. So he took up a newspaper, and occupied himself therewith, until his wife had undressed and put their two oldest children to bed. As she returned from the adjoining room, where they slept, Ellis looked earnestly into her face, to see what hope there was for him in its expression. Her lips were drawn closely together, her brows slightly contracted, and her countenance had a fretful, discontented expression. He sighed inwardly, and resumed the perusal of his newspaper; or, rather, affected to resume it, for the words that met his eyes conveyed to his mind no intelligible ideas.

Mrs. Ellis took her work-basket, and commenced sewing, while her husband continued to hold the newspaper before his face. After some ten minutes of silence, the latter made a remark, as a kind of feeler. This was replied to with what sounded more like a grunt than a vocal expression.

"Cara," at length said Ellis, forcing himself to the unpleasant work on hand, "I would like to have a little plain talk with you about my affairs." He tried, in saying this, to seem not to be very serious; but his feelings, which had for some time been on the rack, were too painfully excited to admit of this. He both looked and expressed, in the tones of his voice, the trouble he felt.

Now, just at the moment Ellis said this, his wife was on the eve of making the announcement, in rather a peremptory and dogmatic way, that if he didn't give her the money to buy new parlour carpets, for which she had been asking as much as a year past, she would go and order them, and have the bill sent in to him. All day this subject had been in her mind, and she had argued herself into the belief that her husband was perfectly able, not only to afford her new carpets, but also new parlour furniture; and that his unwillingness to do so arose from a penurious spirit. Such being her state of mind, she was not prepared to see in the words, voice, and look of her husband the real truth that it was so important for her to know. From the beginning of their married life, she had been disposed to spend freely, and he to restrain her. In consequence, there was a kind of feud between them; and now she regarded his words as coming from a desire on his part to make her believe that he was poorer, in the matter of this world's goods, than was really the case. Her reply, therefore, rather pettishly uttered, was -

"Oh! I've heard enough about your affairs. No doubt you are on the verge of bankruptcy. A man who indulges his family to the extent that you do must expect shipwreck with every coming gale."

The change of countenance and exclamation with which this heartless retort was made startled even Cara. Rising quickly to his feet, and flinging upon his wife a look of reproach, Ellis left the room. A moment or two afterwards, the street-door shut after him with a heavy jar.

It was past midnight when he came home, and then he was stupid from drink.

CHAPTER XI

HOW different was it with Wilkinson, when he returned to his wife on the same evening, in a most gloomy, troubled, and desponding state of mind! A review of his affairs had brought little, if any thing, to encourage him. This dead loss of two thousand dollars was more, he felt, than he could bear. Ere this came upon him, there was often great difficulty in making his payments. How should he be able to make them now, with such an extra weight to carry? The thought completely disheartened him.

"I, too, ought to retrench," said he, mentally, his thoughts recurring to the interview which had taken place between him and Ellis. "In fact, I don't see what else is to save me. But how can I ask Mary to give up her present style of living? How can I ask her to move into a smaller house? to relinquish one of her domestics, and in other respects to deny herself, when the necessity for so doing is wholly chargeable to my folly? It is no use; I can't do it. Every change - every step downwards, would rebuke me. No - no. Upon Mary must not rest the evil consequences of my insane conduct. Let me, alone, suffer."

But how, alone, was he to bear, without sinking beneath the weight, the pressure that was upon him?

With the usual glad smile and heart-warm kiss Wilkinson was greeted on his return home.

"God bless you, Mary!" said he, with much feeling, as he returned his wife's salutation.

Mrs. Wilkinson saw that her husband was inwardly moved to a degree that was unusual. She did not remark thereon, but her manner was gentle, and her tones lower and tenderer than usual, when she spoke to him. But few words passed between them, until the bell rang for tea. While sitting at the table, the voice of Ella was heard, crying.

"Agnes!" called Mrs. Wilkinson, going to the head of the stairs that led down into the kitchen - "I wish you would go up to Ella, she is awake."

The girl answered that she would do as desired, and Mrs. Wilkinson returned to her place at the table.

"Where is Anna?" asked Mr. Wilkinson.

Mrs. Wilkinson smiled cheerfully, as she replied,

"Her month was up to-day, and I concluded to let her go."

"What!" Wilkinson spoke in a quick surprised voice.

"She was little more than a fifth wheel to our coach," was replied; "and fifth wheels can easily be dispensed with."

"But who is to take care of Ella? Who is to do the chamber work? Not you!"

"Don't be troubled about that, my good husband!" was answered with a smile. "Leave all to me. I am the housekeeper."

"You are not strong enough, Mary. You will injure your health."

"My health is more likely to suffer from lack, than from excess of effort. The truth is, I want more exercise than I have been in the habit of taking."

"But the confinement, Mary. Don't you see that the arrangement you propose will tie you down to the house? Indeed, I can't think of it."

"I shall not be confined in-doors any more than I am now. Agnes will take care of the baby whenever I wish to go out."

"There is too much work in this house, Mary'" said Mr. Wilkinson, in a decided way. "You cannot get along with but a single domestic."

"There are only you, and Ella, and I!" Mrs. Wilkinson leaned towards her husband, and looked earnestly into his face. There was an expression on her countenance that was full of meaning; yet its import he did not understand.

"Only you, and Ella, and I?" said he.

"Yes; only we three. Now, I have been wondering all day, John, whether there was any real necessity for just we three having so large a house to live in. I don't think there is. It is an expense for nothing, and makes work for nothing."

"How you talk, Mary!"

"Don't I talk like a sensible woman?" said the young wife, smiling.

"We can't go into a smaller house, dear."

"And why not, pray?"

"Our position in society" -

Mr. Wilkinson did not finish the sentence; for he knew that argument would be lost on his wife.

"We are not rich," said Mrs. Wilkinson.

"No one knows that better than myself," replied the husband, with more feeling than he meant to exhibit.

"And, if the truth were known, are living at an expense beyond what we can afford. Speak out plainly, dear, and say if this is not the case."

"I shouldn't just like to say that," returned Wilkinson; yet his tone of voice belied his words.

"It is just as I supposed," said Mrs. Wilkinson, growing more serious. "Why have you not confided in me? Why have you not spoken freely to me on this subject, John? Am I not your wife? And am I not ready to bear all things and to suffer all things for your sake?"

"You are too serious Mary, - too serious by far. I have not said that there was any thing wrong in my circumstances. I have not said that it was necessary to reduce our expenses."

"No matter, dear. We are, by living in our present style, expending several hundred dollars a year more than is necessary. This is useless. Do you not say so yourself?"

It is certainly useless to spend more than is necessary to secure comfort."

"And wrong to spend more than we can afford?"

"Undoubtedly."

"Then let us take a smaller house, John, by all means. I shall feel so much better contented."

It was some time before Wilkinson replied. When he did so, he spoke with unusual emotion.

"Ah, my dear wife!" said he, leaning towards her and grasping her hand; "you know not how great a load you have taken from my heart. The change you suggest is necessary; yet I never could have urged it; never could have asked you to give up this for an humbler dwelling. How much rather would I elevate you to a palace!"

"My husband! Why, why have you concealed this from me? It was not true kindness," said Mrs. Wilkinson, in a slightly chiding voice. "It is my province to stand, sustainingly, by your side; not to hang upon you, a dead weight."

But we will not repeat all that was said. Enough that, ere the evening, spent in earnest conversation, closed, all the preliminaries of an early removal and reduction of expenses were settled, and, when Wilkinson retired for the night, it was in a hopeful spirit. Light had broken through a rift in the dark cloud which had so suddenly loomed up; and he saw, clearly, the way of escape from the evil that threatened to overwhelm him.

T. S. Arthur

CHAPTER XII

TWELVE o'clock of the day on which Ellis was to return the two hundred dollars borrowed of Wilkinson came, and yet he did not appear at the store of the latter, who had several payments to make, and depended on receiving the amount due from his friend.

"Has Mr. Ellis been here?" asked Wilkinson of his clerk, coming in about noon from a rather fruitless effort to obtain money.

The clerk replied in the negative.

"Nor sent over his check for two hundred dollars?"

"No, sir."

"Step down to his store, then, if you please, and say to him from me that he mustn't forget the sum to be returned to-day, as I have two notes yet in bank. Say also, that if he has any thing over, I shall be glad to have the use of it."

The clerk departed on his errand. In due time he returned, but with no money in his possession.

"Did you see Mr. Ellis?" asked Wilkinson.

"No, sir," was replied. "He hasn't been at the store to-day."

"Not to-day!"

"No, sir."

"What's the matter? Is he sick?"

"His clerk didn't say."

Taking up his hat, Wilkinson left his store hurriedly. In a few minutes he entered that of his friend.

"Where is Mr. Ellis?" he inquired.

"I don't know, sir," was answered by the clerk.

"Has he been here this morning?"

"No, sir."

"He must be sick. Have you sent to his house to make inquiry?"

"Not yet. I have expected him all the morning."

"He was here yesterday?"

"Not until late in the afternoon."

"Indeed! Did he complain of not being well?"

"No, sir. But he didn't look very well."

There was something in the manner of the clerk which

T. S. Arthur

Wilkinson did not understand clearly at first. But all at once it flashed upon his mind that Ellis might, in consequence of some trouble with his wife, have suddenly abandoned himself to drink. With this thought came the remembrance of what had passed between them two days before; and this but confirmed his first impression.

"If Mr. Ellis comes in," said he, after some moments of hurried thought, "tell him that I would like to see him."

The clerk promised to do so.

"Hadn't you better send to his house?" suggested Wilkinson, as he turned to leave the store. "He may be sick."

"I will do so," replied the clerk, and Wilkinson retired, feeling by no means comfortable. By this time it was nearly one o'clock, and six or seven hundred dollars were yet required to make him safe for that day's payments. The failure of Ellis to keep his promise laid upon him an additional burden, and gradually caused a feeling of despondency to creep in upon him. Instead of making a new and more earnest effort to raise the money, he went back to his store, and remained there for nearly half an hour, in a brooding, disheartened state of mind. A glance at the clock, with the minute-hand alarmingly near the figure 2, startled him at length from his dreaming inactivity; and he went forth again to raise, if possible, the money needed to keep his name from commercial dishonour. He was success-ful; but there were only fifteen minutes in his favour when the exact sum he needed was made up, and his notes taken out of bank.

Two o'clock was Mr. Wilkinson's dinner hour, and he had always, before, so arranged his bank business as to have his notes taken up long enough before that time to be ready to leave promptly for home. But for the failure of Ellis to keep his promise, it would have been so on this day.

"It's hardly worth while to go home now," said he, as he closed his cash and bill books, after making some required entries therein. "Mary has given me over long ago. And, besides, I don't feel in the mood of mind to see her just now. I can't look cheerful, to save me; and I have already called too many shadows to her face to darken it with any more. By evening I will recover myself, and then can meet her with a brighter countenance. No, I won't go home now. I'll stop around to Elder's, and get a cut of roast beef."

Wilkinson had taken up his hat, and was moving down the store, when a suggestion that came to his mind made him pause. It was this:

"But is not Mary waiting for me, and will not my absence for the whole day cause her intense anxiety and alarm? I ought to go home."

And now began an argument in his thoughts. The fact was, a sense of exhaustion of body and depression of spirits had followed the effort and trouble of the day, and Wilkinson felt a much stronger desire for something stimulating to drink than he did for food. Elder's was a drinking as well as an eating-house; and in deciding to go there, instead of returning home, the real influence, although he did not perceive it to be so, was the craving felt for a glass of brandy. And now came the conflict between appetite and an instinctive

T. S. Arthur

sense of what was due both to himself and his wife.

"It will only put her to trouble if I go home now." Thus he sought to justify himself in doing what his better sense clearly condemned as wrong.

"It will rather relieve her from trouble," was quickly answered to this.

For a little while Wilkinson stood undecided, then slowly retired to a remote part of the store, took off his hat, and sat down to debate the point at issue in his mind more coolly.

"I will go home early," said he to himself.

"Why not go home now?" was instantly replied.

"It is too late; Mary has given me up long ago."

"She will be extremely anxious."

"I can explain all."

"Better do it now than two or three hours later: poor Mary has suffered enough already."

This last suggestion caused the image of his wife to come up before the mind of Wilkinson very distinctly. He saw, now, her smile of winning love; now, the sad drooping of her countenance, as he turned to leave her alone for an evening; now, the glance of anxiety and fear with which she so often greeted his return; and now, her pale, grief-stricken face, after some one of his too many lapses from the right way. And, in imagination, his thoughts went to his home in the present moment. What did he see? A waiting, anxious, troubled wife, now sitting with fixed and dreamy eyes; now moving about with restless steps; and now standing at the street-door, eagerly straining her eyes to see in the distance his approaching form. With such images of his wife came no repulsive thought to the mind of Wilkinson. Ever loving, tender, patient, forbearing, and true-hearted had Mary been. Not once in the whole of their married life had she jarred the chord that bound them together, with a touch of discord. He could only think of her, therefore, with love, and a feeling of attraction; and this it was that saved him in the present hour. Starting up suddenly, he said, "I will go home: why have I hesitated an instant? My poor Mary! Heaven knows you have already suffered enough through my short-comings and wanderings from the way of right and duty. I am walking a narrow path, with destruction on either hand: if I get over safely, it will be through you as my sustaining angel."

A skilful limner, at least in this instance, was the imagination of Wilkinson. Much as it had been pictured to his thoughts was the scene at home. Poor Mary! with what trembling anxiety did she wait and hope for her husband's coming, after the usual hour for his return had passed. Now she sat motionless, gazing on some painful image that was presented to her mind; now she moved about the room from an unquietness of spirit that would not let her be still; and now she bent her ear towards the street, and listened almost breathlessly for the sound of her husband's footsteps. Thus the time passed from two until three o'clock, the dinner yet unserved.

"Oh, what can keep him away so long?"

T. S. Arthur

How many, many times was this spoken audibly! Now her heart beat with a quick, panting motion, as the thought of some accident to her husband flitted through the mind of Mrs. Wilkinson; now its irregular motion subsided, and it lay almost still, with a heavy pressure; for the fear lest he had again been tempted from the path of sobriety came with its deep and oppressive shadow.

And thus the lingering moments passed. Three o'clock came, and yet Mr. Wilkinson was absent.

"I can bear this suspense no longer," said the unhappy wife. "Something has happened."

And as she said this, she went quickly into her chamber to put into execution some suddenly-formed resolution. Opening a wardrobe, she took therefrom her bonnet and a shawl. But, ere she had thrown the latter around her shoulders, she paused, with the words on her lips -

"If business should have detained him at his store, how will my appearance there affect him? I must think of that. I do not want him to feel that I have lost confidence in him."

While Mrs. Wilkinson stood, thus musing, her ear caught the sound of her husband's key in the lock of the street-door. How quickly were her bonnet and shawl returned to their places! How instant and eager were her efforts to suppress all signs of anxiety at the prolonged absence!

"He must not see that I have been over-anxious," she murmured.

The street-door closed; Mr. Wilkinson's well-known tread sounded along the passage and up the stairway. With what an eager discrimination was the ear of his wife bent towards him for a sign that would indicate the condition in which he returned to her! How breathless was her suspense! A few moments, and the door of her room opened.

"Why, John!" said she, with a pleasant smile, and a tone so well disguised that it betrayed little of the sea of agitation below - "what has kept you so late? I was really afraid something had happened. Have you been sick; or did business detain you?"

"It was business, dear," replied Mr. Wilkinson, as he took the hand which Mary placed within his. The low, nervous tremour of that hand he instantly perceived, and as instantly comprehended its meaning. She had been deeply anxious, but was now seeking to conceal this from him. He understood it all, and was touched by the fact.

"I ought to have sent you word," said he, as he kissed her with more than usual tenderness of manner. "It was wrong in me. But I've been very hard put to it to take up my notes, and didn't succeed until near the closing of bank hours. I loaned Ellis some money, which he was to return to me to-day; but his failing to do so put me to a good deal of inconvenience."

"Oh, I'm sorry," was the sympathizing response. "But how came Mr. Ellis to disappoint you?"

"I don't exactly know. He hasn't been at his store to-day."

"Is he sick?"

"Worse, I'm afraid."

"How, worse?"

"His habits have not been very good of late."

"Oh! how sad! His poor wife!"

This was an almost involuntary utterance on the part of Mrs. Wilkinson.

"Her poor husband, rather say," was the reply. "The fact is, if Ellis goes to ruin, it will be his wife's fault. She has no sympathy with him, no affectionate consideration for him. A thoroughly selfish woman, she merely regards the gratification of her own desires, and is ever making home repulsive, instead of attractive."

"You must be mistaken."

"No. Ellis often complains to me of her conduct."

"Why, John! I can scarcely credit such a thing."

"Doubtless it is hard for *you* to imagine any woman guilty of such unwifelike conduct. Yet such is the case. Many a night has Ellis spent at a tavern, which, but for Cara's unamiable temper, would have been spent at home."

"Ah! she will have her reward," sighed Mrs. Wilkinson.

"And you yours," was the involuntary but silent ejaculation of Wilkinson.

Ere further remark was made, the dinner-bell rang, and Mr. Wilkinson and his wife repaired to the dining-room.

It was not possible for the former to endure the pressure that was on his feelings without letting the fact of its existence betray itself in his countenance; and Mary, whose eyes were scarcely a moment from her husband's face, soon saw that his mind was ill at ease.

"How much did Mr. Ellis borrow of you?" she asked, soon after they had taken their places at the table.

"Two hundred dollars," was replied.

"No more?" The mind of Mrs. Wilkinson was evidently relieved, at knowing the smallness of the sum.

"True, it isn't much," said Wilkinson. "But even a small sum is of great importance when we have a good deal to pay, and just lack that amount, after gathering in all our available resources. And that was just my position to-day." Why didn't you call on me?" Mary smiled, with evident meaning as she said this.

"On you!" Wilkinson looked at her with a slight air of surprise.

"Yes, on me. I think I could have made you up that sum."

"You!"

A bright gleam went over the face of Mrs. Wilkinson, as she saw the surprise of her husband.

"Yes, me. Why not? You have always been liberal in your supplies of money, and it is by no means wonderful that I should have saved a little. The fact is, John, I've never spent my entire income; I always made it a point of conscience to keep as far below it as possible."

"Mary!" Beyond this simple ejaculation, Wilkinson could not go, but sat, with his eyes fixed wonderingly on the face of his wife.

"It is true, dear," she answered, in her loving gentle way. "I haven't counted up lately; but, if I do not err, I have twice the sum you needed to-day; and, what is more, the whole is at your service. So don't let this matter of Ellis's failure to return you the sum borrowed, trouble you in the least. If it never comes back to you, the loss will be made up in another quarter."

It was some moments before Wilkinson could make any answer. At last, dropping the knife and fork which he held in his hands, he started from his place, and coming round to where his wife sat, drew his arms around her, and as he pressed his lips to hers, said with an unsteady voice -

"God bless you, Mary! You are an angel!"

Had she not her reward in that happy moment? Who will say nay?

CHAPTER XIII

ON the morning that followed the fruitless attempt of Henry Ellis to make his wife comprehend the necessity that existed for an immediate reduction in their household expenditures, he did not get up until nearly ten o'clock. For at least an hour before rising, he was awake, suffering in both body and mind; for the night's debauch had left him, as was usually the case, with a most violent headache. During all the time he heard, at intervals, the voice of Cara in the adjoining, talking to or scolding at the children; but not once during the time did she come into the chamber where he lay. He felt it as a total want of interest or affection on her part. He had done wrong; he felt that; yet, at the same time, he also felt that Cara had her share of the blame to bear. If she had only manifested some feeling for him, some interest in him, he would have been softened; but, as she did not, by keeping entirely away, show that she thought or cared for him, the pure waters of right feeling, that were gushing up in his mind, were touched with the gall of bitterness.

Rising at length, Ellis began dressing himself, purposely making sufficient noise to reach the ears of his wife. But she did not make her appearance.

Two doors led from the chamber in which he was. One communicated with the adjoining room, used as a

T. S. Arthur

nursery, and the other with the passage. After Ellis had dressed and shaved himself, he was, for a short time, undecided whether to enter the nursery, in which were his wife and children, or to pass through the other door, and leave the house without seeing them.

"I shall only get my feelings hurt," said he, as he stood debating the point. "It's a poor compensation for trouble and the lack of domestic harmony, to get drunk, I know; and I ought to be, and am, ashamed of my own folly. Oh dear! what is to become of me? Why will not Cara see the evil consequences of the way she acts upon her husband? If I go to destruction, and the chances are against me, the sin will mainly rest upon her. Yet why should I say this? Am I not man enough to keep sober? Yes" - thus he went on talking to himself - "but if she will not act in some sort of unity with me, I shall be ruined in my business. It will never do to maintain our present expensive mode of living; and she will never hear to a change."

Just at this moment an angry exclamation from the lips of Mrs. Ellis came sharply on the ears of her husband, followed by the whipping and crying of one of the children, who had, as far as Ellis could gather, from what was said, overset his mother's work-basket.

"No use for me to go in there," muttered the unhappy man. "I shall only increase the storm; and I've had storms enough!"

So he went from the chamber by way of the passage, descended to the entry below, and, taking up his hat, left the house.

Now, of all things in the world, in the peculiar state of

body and mind in which Ellis then was, did he want a good strong cup of coffee at his own table, and a kind, forbearing, loving wife to set it before him. These would have given to his body and to his mind just what both needed, for the trials and temptations of the day; and they would have saved him, at least for the day, perhaps for life; for the pivot upon which the whole of a man's future destiny turns is often small, and scarcely noticed.

As Ellis stepped from his door, and received the fresh air upon his face and in his lungs, he was instantly conscious of a want in his system, and a craving for something to supply that want. Having taken no breakfast, the feeling was not to be wondered at. Ellis understood its meaning, in part, and took the nearest way to an eating-house where he ordered something to eat. For him, it was the most natural thing in the world, under the circumstances, to call for something at the bar while his breakfast was preparing. He felt better after taking a glass of brandy.

Ellis had finished his breakfast, and was standing at the bar with a second glass of liquor in his hand, when he was accosted in a familiar manner by the same individual who had lured Wilkinson to the gaming-table.

"Ah, my boy! how are you?" said Carlton, grasping the hand of Ellis and shaking it heartily.

"Glad to see you, 'pon my word! Where do you keep yourself?"

"You'll generally find me at my store during business hours," replied Ellis.

"What do you call business hours?" was asked by Carlton.

"From eight or nine in the morning until six or seven in the evening."

"Yes - yes - yes! With you as with every other 'business' man I know. Business every thing - living nothing. You'll get rich, I suppose; but, by the time your sixty or a hundred thousand dollars are safely invested in real estate or good securities, health will have departed, never to return."

"Not so bad as that, I presume," returned Ellis.

"How can it be otherwise? The human body is not made of iron and steel; and, if it were, it would never stand the usage it receives from some men, you among the number. For what are the pure air and bright sunshine made? To be enjoyed only by the birds and beasts? Man is surely entitled to his share; and if he neglects to take it, he does so to his own injury. You don't look well. In fact, I never saw you look worse; and I noticed, when I took your hand, that it was hot. Now, my good fellow! this is little better than suicide on your part; and if I do not mistake, you are too good a Christian to be guilty of self-murder. Why don't you ride out and take the air? You ought to do this daily."

"Too expensive a pleasure for me," said Ellis. "In the first place, with me time is money, and, in the second place, I have no golden mint-drops to exchange for fast horses."

"I have a fine animal at your service," replied the tempter. "Happy to let you use him at any time."

"Much obliged for the offer; and when I can run away from business for a few hours, will avail myself of it."

"What do you say to a ride this morning? I'm going a few miles over into Jersey, and should like your company above all things."

"I hardly think I can leave the store to-day," replied Ellis. "Let me see: have I any thing in the way of a note to take up? I believe not."

"You say yes, then?"

"I don't know about that. It doesn't just seem right."

"Nonsense! It is wonderful how this business atmosphere does affect a man's perceptions! He can see nothing but the dollar. Every thing is brought down to a money valuation."

We will not trace the argument further. Enough that the tempter was successful, and that Ellis, instead of going to his store, rode out with Carlton.

He was not, of course, home at his usual dinner-hour. It was between three and four o'clock when he appeared at his place of business, the worse for his absence, in almost every sense of the word. He had been drinking, until he was half stupid, and was a loser at the gaming-table of nearly six hundred dollars. A feeble effort was made by him to go into an examination of the business of the day; but he found it impossible to fix his mind thereon, and so gave up the attempt. He remained at his store until ready to close up for the day, and then turned his steps homeward.

By this time he was a good deal sobered, and sadder for his sobriety; for, as his mind became clearer, he remembered, with more vividness, the events of the day, and particularly the fact of having lost several hundred dollars to his pretended friend, Carlton.

"Whither am I going? Where is this to end?" was his shuddering ejaculation, as the imminent peril of his position most vividly presented itself.

How hopelessly he wended his reluctant way homeward! There was nothing to lean upon there. No strength of ever-enduring love, to be, as it were, a second self to him in his weakness. No outstretched arm to drag him, with something of super-human power, out of the miry pit into which he had fallen; but, instead, an indignant hand to thrust him farther in.

"God help me!" he sighed, in the very bitterness of a hopeless spirit; "for there is no aid in man."

Ah! if, in his weakness, he had only leaned, in true dependence, on Him he thus asked to help him; if he had but resisted the motions of evil in himself, as sins against his Maker, and resisted them in a determined spirit, he need not have fallen; strength would, assuredly, have been given.

The nearer Ellis drew to his home, the more unhappy he felt at the thought of meeting his wife. After having left the house without seeing her in the morning, and then remaining from home all day, he had no hope of a kind reception.

"It's no use!" he muttered to himself, stopping suddenly, when within a square of his house. "I can't meet Cara; she will look coldly at me, or frown, or speak cutting words; and I'm in no state of mind to bear any thing patiently just now. I've done wrong, I know - very wrong; but I don't want it thrown into my face. Oh, dear! I am beset within and without, behind and before and there is little hope for me."

Overcoming this state of indecision, Ellis forced himself to go home. On entering the presence of his wife, he made a strong effort to compose himself, and, when he met Cara, he spoke to her in a cheerful tone of voice. How great an effort it cost him to do this, considering all the circumstances by which he was surrounded, the reader may easily imagine. And what was his reception?

"Found your way home at last!"

These were the words with which Cara received her husband; and they were spoken in a sharp, deriding tone of voice. The day's doubt, suspense, and suffering, had not quieted the evil spirit in her heart. She was angry with her husband, and could not restrain its expression.

A bitter retort trembled on the tongue of Ellis; but he checked its utterance, and, turning from his wife, took one of his children in his arms. The sphere of innocence that surrounded the spirit of that child penetrated his heart, and touched his feelings with an emotion of tenderness.

"Oh, wretched man that I am!" he sighed, in the bitterness of a repentant and self-upbraiding spirit. "So much dependent on me, and yet as weak as a reed swaying in the wind."

How much that weak, tempted, suffering man, just trembling on the brink of destruction, needed a true-hearted, forbearing, long-suffering wife! Such a one might - yes, would - have saved him. By the strong cords of love she would have held him to her side.

Several times Ellis tried to interest Cara in conversation; but to every remark she replied only in monosyllables. In fact she was angry with him, and, not feeling kindly, she would not speak kindly. All day she had suffered deeply on his account. A thousand fears had harassed her mind. She had even repented of her unkindness towards him, and resolved to be more forbearing in the future. For more than an hour she kept the table waiting at dinner time, and was so troubled at his absence, that she felt no inclination to touch food.

"I'm afraid I am not patient enough with him," she sighed, as better feelings warmed in her heart. "I was always a little irritable. But I will try to do better. If he were not so close about money, I could be more patient."

While such thoughts were passing through the mind of Mrs. Ellis, a particular friend, named Mrs. Claxton, called to see her.

"Why, bless me, Cara! what's the matter?" exclaimed this lady, as she took the hand of Mrs. Ellis. "You look dreadful. Haven't been sick, I hope?"

"No, not sick in body," was replied.

"Sick in mind. The worst kind of sickness. No serious trouble, I hope?"

There was a free, off-hand, yet insinuating manner about Mrs. Claxton, that, while it won the confidence of a certain class of minds, repulsed others. Mrs. Ellis, who had no great skill in reading character, belonged to the former class; and Mrs. Claxton was, therefore as just said, a particular friend, and in a certain sense a confidante.

"The old trouble," replied Mrs. Ellis to the closing question of her friend.

"With your husband?"

"Yes. He pinches me in money matters so closely, and grumbles so eternally at what he calls my extravagance, that I'm out of all patience. Last evening, just as I was about telling him that he must give me new parlour carpets, he, divining, I verily believe, my thoughts, cut off every thing, by saying, in a voice as solemn as the grave - 'Cara, I would like to have a little plain talk with you about my affairs.' I flared right up. I couldn't have helped it, if I'd died for it the next minute."

"Well; what then?"

"Oh! the old story. Of course he got angry, and went off like a streak of lightning. I cried half the evening, and then went to bed. I don't know how late it was when he came home. This morning, when I got up, he was sleeping as heavy as a log. It was near ten o'clock when I heard him moving about in our chamber, but I did not go in. He had got himself into a huff, and I was determined to let him get himself out of it. Just as I supposed he would come into the nursery, where I was sitting with the children, awaiting his lordship's pleasure to appear for breakfast, he opens the door into the passage, and walks himself off."

"Without his breakfast?"

"Yes, indeed. And I've seen nothing of him since."

"That's bad," said the friend. "A little tiff now and then is all well enough in its place. But this is too serious."

"So I feel it. Yet what am I to do?"

"You will have to manage better than this."

"Manage?"

"Yes. I never have scenes of this kind with my husband."

"He's not so close with you as Henry is with me. He isn't so mean, if I must speak plainly, in money matters."

"Well, I don't know about that. He isn't perfect by many degrees. One of his faults, from the beginning, has been a disposition to dole out my allowance of money with a very sparing hand. I bore this for some years, but it fretted me; and was the source of occasional misunderstandings that were very unpleasant."

Mrs. Claxton paused.

"Well; what remedy did you apply?" asked Mrs. Ellis.

"A very simple one. I took what he was pleased to give

me, and if it didn't hold out, I bought what I needed, and had the bills sent in to the store."

"Capital!" exclaimed Mrs. Ellis. "Just what I have been thinking of. And it worked well?"

"To a charm."

"What did Mr. Claxton say when the bills came in?"

"He looked grave, and said I would ruin him; but, of course, paid them."

"Is that the way you got your new carpets?"

"Yes."

"And your new blinds?"

"Yes."

"Well, I declare! But doesn't Mr. Claxton diminish your allowances of money?"

"Yes, but his credit is as good as his money. I never pay for dry goods, shoes, or groceries. The bills are all sent in to him."

"And he never grumbles?"

"I can't just say that. It isn't a week since he assured me, with the most solemn face in the world, that if I didn't manage to keep the family on less than I did, he would certainly be ruined in his business."

"The old story."

"Yes. I've heard it so often, that it goes in at one ear and out at the other."

"So have I. But I like your plan amazingly, and mean to adopt it. In fact, something of the kind was running through my head yesterday."

"Do so; and you will save yourself a world of petty troubles. I find that it works just right."

This advice of her friend Mrs. Ellis pondered all the afternoon, and, after viewing the matter on all sides, deliberately concluded to act in like manner. Yet, for all this, she could not conquer a certain angry feeling that rankled towards her husband, and, in spite of sundry half formed resolutions to meet him, when he returned, in a kind manner, her reception of him was such as the reader has seen.

CHAPTER XIV

THE turning-point with Ellis had nearly come. It required, comparatively, little beyond the weight of a feather to give preponderance to the scale of evil influences. Cara's reception, as shown in the last chapter, was no worse than he had anticipated, yet it hurt him none the less; for unkind words from her were always felt as blows, and coldness as the pressure upon his heart of an icy hand. In the love of his children, who were very fond of him, he sought a kind of refuge. Henry, his oldest child, was a bright, intelligent boy between eight and nine years of age; and Kate, between six and seven, was a sweet-tempered, affectionate little girl, who scarcely ever left her father's side when he was in the house.

At the tea-table, only the children's voices were heard: they seemed not to perceive the coldness that separated their parents. After supper, Mr. Ellis went up into the nursery with Henry and Kate, and was chatting pleasantly with them, when their mother, who had remained behind to give some directions to a servant, came into the room.

"Come!" said she, in rather a sharp voice, as she entered, "it is time you were in bed."

"Papa is telling us a story," returned Kate, in a pleading

T. S. Arthur

tone: "just let us wait until he is done."

"I've got no time to wait for stories. Come!" said the mother, imperatively.

"Papa will soon be done," spoke up Henry.

"It's early yet, mother," said Ellis; "let them sit up a little while. I'm away all day, and don't see much of them."

"I want them to go to bed now," was the emphatic answer. "It's their bed-time, and I wish them out of the way, so that I can go to work. If you'd had their noise and confusion about you all day, as I have, you'd be glad to see them in their beds."

"You'll have to go," said Mr. Ellis, in a tone of disappointment that he could not conceal. "But get up early to-morrow morning, and I will tell you the rest of the story. Don't cry, dear!" And Mr. Ellis kissed tenderly his little girl, in whose eyes the tears were already starting.

Slowly, and with sad faces, the children turned to obey their mother, who, not for a moment relenting, spoke to them sharply for their lack of prompt obedience. They went crying up-stairs, and she scolding.

The moment the door of the nursery closed upon the retiring forms of the children, Mr. Ellis started to his feet with an impatient exclamation, and commenced pacing the room with rapid steps.

"Temptations without and storms within," said he, bitterly. "Oh, that I had the refuge of a quiet home, and the sustaining heart and wise counsels of a loving wife!"

By the time Mrs. Ellis had undressed the children and got them snugly in bed, her excited feelings were, in a measure, calmed; and from calmer feelings flowed the natural result - clearer thoughts. Then came the conviction of having done wrong, and regret for a hasty and unkind act.

"He sees but little of them, it is true," she murmured, "and I might have let them remain up a little while longer, I'm too thoughtless, sometimes; but I get so tired of their noise and confusion, which is kept up all day long."

And then she sighed.

Slowly, and with gentler feelings, Mrs. Ellis went down-stairs. Better thoughts were in her mind, and she was inwardly resolving to act towards her husband in a different spirit from that just manifested. On entering the nursery, where she had left him, she was not a little disappointed to find that he was not there.

"It isn't possible that he has gone out!" was her instant mental ejaculation; and she passed quickly into the adjoining chamber to see if he were there. It was empty.

For some time Mrs. Ellis stood in deep abstraction of mind; then, as a sigh heaved her bosom, she moved from the chamber and went down-stairs. A glance at the hat-stand confirmed her fears; her husband had left the house.

"Ah, me!" she sighed. "It is hard to know how to get along with him. If every thing isn't just to suit his fancy, off he goes. I might humour him more than I do, but it isn't in me to humour any one. And for a man to want to be humoured! Oh, dear! oh, dear! this is a wretched way to live; it will kill me in the end. These men expect their own way in every thing, and if they don't get it, then there is trouble. I'm not fit to be Henry's wife. He ought to have married a woman with less independence of spirit; one who would have been the mere creature of his whims and fancies."

Mrs. Ellis, with a troubled heart, went up to the room where so many of her lonely evening hours were spent. Taking her work-basket, she tried to sew; but her thoughts troubled her so, that she finally sought refuge therefrom in the pages of an exciting romance.

The realizing power of imagination in Ellis was very strong. While he paced the floor after his wife and children had left the room, there came to him such a vivid picture of the coldness and reserve that must mark the hours of that evening, if they were passed with Cara, that he turned from it with a sickening sense of pain. Under the impulse of that feeling he left the house, but with no purpose as to where he was going.

For as long, perhaps, as half an hour, Ellis walked the street, his mind, during most of the time, pondering the events of the day. His absence from business was so much lost, and would throw double burdens on the morrow, for, besides the sum of two hundred dollars to be returned to Wilkinson, he had a hundred to make up for another friend who had accommodated him. But where was the money to come from? In the matter of borrowing, Ellis had never done much, and his resources in that line were small. His losses at the gaming-table added so much to the weight of discouragement under which he suffered!

"You play well." Frequently had the artful tempter, Carlton, lured his victim on by this and other similar expressions, during the time he had him in his power; and thus flattered, Ellis continued at cards until repeated losses had so far sobered him as to give sufficient mental resolution to enable him to stop.

Now, these expressions returned to his mind, and their effect upon him was manifested in the thought, -

"If I hadn't been drinking, he would have found in me a different antagonist altogether."

It was an easy transition from this state of mind to another. It was almost natural for the wish to try his luck again at cards to be formed; particularly as he was in great need of money, and saw no legitimate means of getting the needed supply.

The frequency with which Ellis had spent his evenings abroad made him acquainted with many phases of city life hidden from ordinary observers. Idle curiosity had more than once led him to visit certain gambling-houses on a mere tour of observation; and, during these visits, he had each time been tempted to try a game or two, in which cases little had been lost or won. The motive for winning did not then exist in tempting strength; and, besides, Ellis was naturally a cautious man. Now, however, the motive did exist.

"Yes, I do play well," said he, mentally answering the remembered compliment of Carlton, "and but for your stealing away my brains with liquor, you would have found me a different kind of antagonist."

Ellis had fifty dollars in his pocket. This sum was the amount of the day's sales of goods in his store. Instead of leaving the money in his fire-closet, he had taken it with him, a sort of dim idea being in his mind that, possibly, it might be wanted for some such purpose as now contemplated. So he was all prepared for a trial of his skill; and the trial was made. To one of the haunts of iniquity before visited in mere reprehensible curiosity, he now repaired with the deliberate purpose of winning money to make up for losses already sustained, and to provide for the next day's payments. He went in with fifty dollars in his pocket-book; at twelve o'clock he left the place perfectly sober, and the winner of three hundred dollars. Though often urged to drink, he had, knowing his weakness, firmly declined in every instance.

Cara, he found, as usual on returning home late at night, asleep. He sought his pillow without disturbing her, and lay for a long time with his thoughts busy among golden fancies. In a few hours he had won three hundred dollars, and that from a player of no common skill.

"Yes, yes, Carlton said true. I play well." Over and over did Ellis repeat this, as he lay with his mind too much excited for sleep.

Wearied nature yielded at last. His dreams repeated the incidents of the evening, and reconstructed them into new and varied forms. When he awoke, at day-dawn, from his restless slumber, it took but a short time for his thoughts to arrange themselves into a purpose, and that purpose was to seek out Carlton as the first business of the day, and win back the evidence of debt that he had against him.

The meeting of Ellis and his wife at the breakfast-table had less of coldness and reserve in it than their meeting at tea-time. No reference was made to the previous evening, nor to the fact of his having remained out to a late hour.

It was the intention of Ellis, on leaving his house after breakfast, to repair to his store and make some preliminary arrangements for the day before hunting up Carlton; but on his way thither, his appetite constrained him to enter a certain drinking-house just for a single glass of brandy to give his nerves their proper tension.

"Ah! how are you, my boy?" exclaimed Carlton, who was there before him, advancing as he spoke, and offering his hand in his usual frank way.

"Glad to meet you!" returned Ellis. "Just the man I wished to see. Take a drink?"

"I don't care if I do."

And the two men moved up to the bar. When they turned away, Carlton drew his arm familiarly within that of Ellis, and bending close to his ear, said - "You wish to take up your due-bills, I presume?

"You guess my wishes precisely," was the answer.

"Well, I shall be pleased to have you cancel them. Are you prepared to do it this morning?"

"I am - in the way they were created."

A gleam of satisfaction lit up the gambler's face, which was partly turned from Ellis; but he shrugged his shoulders, and said, in an altered voice - "I'm most afraid to try you again."

"We're pretty well matched, I know," said the victim. "If you decline, of course the matter ends."

"I never like to be bantered," returned Carlton. "If a man were to dare me to jump from the housetop, it would be as much as I could do to restrain myself."

"I've got three hundred in my pocket," said Ellis, "and I'm prepared to see the last dollar of it."

"Good stuff in you, my boy!" and Carlton laid his hand upon his shoulder in a familiar way. "It would hardly be fair not to give you a chance to get back where you were. So here's for you, win or lose, sink or swim."

And the two men left the tavern together. We need not follow them, nor describe the contest that ensued. The result has already been anticipated by the reader. A few hours sufficed to strip Ellis of his three hundred dollars, and increase his debts to the gambler nearly double the former amount.

CHAPTER XV

MRS. ELLIS knew, by the appearance of her husband, that he had not been drinking on the night previous, late as he had remained away. This took a weight from her feelings, and relieved her mind from self-upbraidings that would have haunted her all the day. After breakfast her mind began to ponder what Mrs. Claxton had said on the day previous, and the more she thought of her advice and example, the more she felt inclined to adopt a similar course of action. On new Brussels carpets she had, long ago, set her heart, and already worried her husband about them past endurance. To obtain his consent to the purchase, she felt to be hopeless.

"I must get them in this way, or not at all. So much is clear." Thus she communed with herself. "He's able enough to pay the bill; if I had any doubts of that, the matter would be settled; but I have none."

With the prospect of getting the long coveted carpets, came an increased desire for their possession.

In imagination Mrs. Ellis saw them already on the floor. For some hours there was a struggle in her mind. Then the tempter triumphed. She dressed herself, and went out for the purpose of making a selection. From this moment she did not hesitate. Calling at a

T. S. Arthur

well-known carpet warehouse, she made her selection, and directed the bill, after the carpet was made and put down, to be sent in to her husband. The price of the carpet she chose was two dollars and a quarter a yard; and the whole bill, including that of the upholsterer, would reach a hundred and sixty dollars.

When Mrs. Ellis returned home, after having consummated her purpose, the thought of her beautiful carpet gave her far less pleasure than she had anticipated. In every wrong act lies its own punishment. Uneasiness of mind follows as a sure consequence. From the idea of her beautiful parlours, her mind would constantly turn to her husband.

"What *will* he say?"

Ah! if she could only have answered that question satisfactorily!

"I will be so good, I will disarm him with kindness. I will humour him in every thing. I will not give him a chance to be angry."

For a while this idea pleased the mind of Mrs. Ellis. But it only brought a temporary respite to the uneasiness produced by her wrong act.

"I'll tell him just what I have done," said she to herself, as the dinner hour approached, and Cara began to look for her husband's return. "He might as well know it now, as in a week; and, besides, it will give him time to prepare for the bill. Yes, that is what I will do."

Still, her mind felt troubled. The act was done, and no way of retreat remained open. The consequences must be met.

The hour for Mr. Ellis to return home at length arrived, and his wife waited his coming with a feeling of troubled suspense such as she had rarely, if ever, before experienced. Smiles, ready to be forced to her countenance, were wreathing themselves in her imagination. She meant to be "*so* good," so loving, so considerate. A particular dish of which he was so fond had been ordered, - it was a month since it had graced their table.

But time moved on. It was thirty minutes past the dinner hour, and he was still away. At last Mrs. Ellis gave him up. A full hour had elapsed, and there was little probability of his return before the close of business for the day. So she sat down with her children to eat the meal which long delay had spoiled, and for which she had now but little appetite.

Wearily passed the afternoon, and, as the usual time for Ellis's appearance drew near, his wife began to look for his coming with feelings of unusual concern. Not concern for him, but for herself. She had pretty well made up her mind to inform him of what she had done, but shrank from the scene which she had every reason to believe would follow.

The twilight had just begun to fall, and Mrs. Ellis, with her babe in her arms, was sitting in one of the parlours, waiting for and thinking of her husband, when she heard his key in the door. He came in, and moving along the entry with a quicker step than usual, went up-stairs. Supposing that, not finding her above, he would come down to the parlours, Mrs. Ellis waited nearly five minutes. Then she followed him up-stairs. Not finding him in the nursery, she passed into their chamber. Here she found him, lying across the bed, on which he had, evidently, thrown himself under some strong excitement, or abandonment, of feeling, for his head was not upon a pillow, and he lay perfectly motionless, as if unconscious of her presence.

"Henry!" She called his name, but he made no answer, nor gave even a sign.

"Henry! Are you sick?"

There was a slight movement of his body, but no reply.

"Henry! Henry!" Mrs. Ellis spoke in tones of anxiety, as she laid her hand upon him. "Speak! What is the matter? Are you sick?"

A long deep sigh was the only answer.

"Why don't you speak, Henry?" exclaimed Mrs. Ellis. "You frighten me dreadfully."

"Don't trouble me just now, if you please," said the wretched man, in a low, half-whispering voice.

"But what ails you, Henry? Are you sick?"

"Yes."

"How? Where? What can I do for you?"

"Nothing!" was faintly murmured.

By this time, Cara began to feel really alarmed. Leaving the room hurriedly, she gave the babe she held in her arms to one of her domestics, and then returned. Bending, now, over her husband, she took one of his hands, and clasping it tightly, said, in a voice of earnest affection that went to the heart of Ellis with electric quickness -

"Do, Henry, say what ails you! Can't I get something for you?"

"I'll feel better in a little while," whispered Ellis.

"Let me send for the doctor."

"Oh, no! no! I'm not so sick as that," was answered. "I only feel a little faint, not having taken any dinner."

"Why did you go without a meal? It is not right to do so. I waited for you so long, and was so disappointed that you did not come."

There was more of tenderness and wife-like interest in Cara's words and manner than had been manifested for a long time, and the feelings of Ellis were touched thereby. Partly raising himself on his elbow, he replied

"I know it isn't right; but I was so much engaged!"

The twilight pervading the room was too feeble to give Mrs. Ellis a distinct view of her husband's countenance. Its true expression, therefore, was veiled.

"You feel better now, do you?" she inquired tenderly.

"Yes, dear," he answered, slightly pressing the hand she had laid in his.

"I will order tea on the table immediately."

And Mrs. Ellis left the room. When she returned, he had risen from the bed, and was sitting in a large chair near one of the windows.

"Are you better, dear?" tenderly inquired Mrs. Ellis.

"Yes, a good deal better," was answered. And the words were truly spoken; for this unlooked-for, kind, even tender reception, had wrought an almost instantaneous change. He had come home with a feeling of despair tugging at his heart. Nothing appeared before him but ruin. Now the light of hope, feeble though were the rays, came glimmering across the darkness of his spirit.

"I am glad to hear it!" was the warm response of Cara. "Oh! it is so wrong for you to neglect your meals. You confine yourself too closely to business. I wanted you to come home to-day particularly, for I had prepared for you, just in the way you like it, such a nice dish of maccaroni."

"It was very thoughtful in you, dear. I wish I had been at home to enjoy it with you."

Tea being announced, Mrs. Ellis arose and said:

"Come; supper is on the table. You must break your long fast."

"First let me wash my hands and face," returned Ellis, who wished to gain time, as well as use all the means, to restore his countenance to a better expression than it wore, ere meeting Cara under the glare of strong lamp light.

A basin was filled for him by his wife, and, after washing his hands and face, he left the chamber with her, and went to the dining-room. Here Cara got a distinct view of her husband's countenance. Many lines of the passion and suffering written there during that, to him, ever-to-be-remembered day, were still visible, and, as Cara read them without comprehending their import, a vague fear came hovering over her heart. Instantly her thoughts turned to what she had been doing, and most sincerely did she repent of the act.

"I will confess it to him, this very night," such was her mental resolution, - "and promise, hereafter never to do aught against his wishes."

Notwithstanding Ellis had taken no dinner, he had little appetite for his evening meal; and the concern of his wife was increased on observing that he merely tasted his food and sipped his tea.

The more than ordinary trouble evinced, as well in the whole manner of Ellis as in the expression of his face and in the tones of his voice, oppressed the heart of Cara. She felt that something more than usual must have occurred to disturb him. Could it be possible that any thing was wrong in his business? The thought caused a low thrill to tremble along her nerves. He had frequently spoken of his affairs as not very prosperous; was always, in fact, making a "sort of a poor mouth." But all this she had understood as meant for effect - as a cover for his opposition to her wish to spend. What if it were all as he had represented?

Such thoughts could not but sober the mind of Mrs.

T. S. Arthur

Ellis, and caused her manner towards her husband to assume an air of tenderness and concern to which it had too long been a stranger. How quickly was this felt by Ellis! How gratefully did his heart respond to his wife's gentler touches on its tensely strung chords!

That evening Henry Ellis spent at home. Not much conversation passed between him and his wife; for the mind of each was too heavily burdened with thoughts of its own to leave room for an interchange of ideas. But the manner of Cara towards her husband was subdued, and even tender; and he felt it as the grateful earth feels the strength-giving impression of the gentle rain. Leaving the past, to the future both their thoughts turned; and both strengthened themselves in good resolutions.

Cara resolved to be a better wife - to be more considerate and more yielding towards her husband. And Ellis resolved to abandon, at every sacrifice the vicious habits he had indulged, - habits which, within a day or two, had led him aside from the path of safety, and conducted him to the brink of a precipice, from which he now started back with a thrilling sense of fear.

More than twenty times during that evening was Cara on the eve of telling her husband about the carpet. But she shrank from the confession.

"In the morning I will do it," was her final conclusion; thus putting off the evil hour. But morning found her no better prepared for the task.

CHAPTER XVI

ALL through the night, the mind of Ellis was haunted with troubled dreams; but, on waking, he felt calm, and good purposes were in his heart. The manner of Cara still being tender and considerate, he went forth feeling the strength of her love, and resolving, for her sake, and the sake of his children, to free himself from his present entanglements, cost what it would.

Seven hundred dollars was the sum he had lost at the gaming-table and for over five hundred of this, Carlton held his obligations, payable on demand. Besides this, he owed on account of temporary loans, from business friends, about an equal amount. Moreover, on that day, a note of three hundred dollars fell due; and in the coming ten days, about a thousand dollars had to be paid into bank. The aggregate of all these obligations, to be met within two weeks, was two thousand three hundred dollars.

As Ellis looked at this formidable amount, and calculated his resources, he felt, for a time, utterly discouraged. But a reaction from this state of feeling came, and he set his mind vigorously to work in devising means for the pressing emergency.

"There is one thing certain," said he to himself, as he pondered the matter. "Carlton will have to wait. So

T. S. Arthur

there are five hundred dollars pushed ahead. I received no value in the case, and shall not hurry myself to make payment."

Even while Ellis thus spoke, a man called and presented the due-bills he had given to the gambler.

"I can't take these up now," was the prompt reply.

"My directions are to collect them forthwith," said the man.

"Mr. Carlton will have to wait my convenience." Ellis spoke with considerable irritation of manner.

"Shall I say so to him?" was asked, in a tone that involved a warning of consequences.

"You can say to him what you please," answered Ellis, sharply.

"Oh! very well!"

The man turned away, and walked towards the door. He paused, however, after going a short distance; stood, as if reflecting, for some moments, and, then came back.

"You had better think over this a little;" said he, in a conciliatory voice. "The debt is, I need not remind you, one of *honour*; and it is neither wise nor safe for a man of business to let such a debt be handed over for legal collection. You understand, I presume?"

The suggestion caused Ellis to start, involuntarily. He saw, at a glance, the dangerous position in which he stood. Only by retaining a fair credit would it be possible for him to surmount his present difficulties; and his credit would be instantly blasted if a suit were brought against him by a man he had now good reasons to believe was known in the community as a gambler.

"You understand me?" repeated the collector, in a tone of marked significance.

Ellis tried to regain his self-possession, and affect indifference. But his feelings were poorly disguised.

"Just say to Mr. Carlton," he replied, "that it is not my purpose to give him any trouble about this matter. I will take up the due-bills. But I have some heavy payments to make, and cannot do it just now."

"When will it be done?"

"That I am unable, just now, to say."

"Can't you give me a part of the money today?"

Ellis shook his head.

"I have notes in bank, and they must take the precedence of all other payments."

"To-morrow, then?"

"I have five hundred dollars to pay to-morrow."

The man's countenance began to lower.

"Just go to Mr. Carlton, if you please, and tell him

what I say. He's a man of common sense; - he will listen to reason."

"My orders to collect were imperative," persisted the man.

"Tell him that you can't collect to-day. That I must and will have time. There now! Go! I've something else to do besides arguing this matter fruitlessly."

The collector turned off with an angry, threatening look. A few minutes after he was gone, and ere the mind of Ellis had recovered its balance, a customer called in and paid a bill of a hundred dollars. This awakened a feeling of confidence; and, in a hopeful spirit, Ellis went forth to make arrangements for the balance of what was wanted for the day. He found no difficulty in procuring the sum he needed, which was four hundred dollars. After taking up his note, he called upon his friend Wilkinson with the two hundred dollars he had failed to return the day before, when, after apologizing for his neglect, he asked him how he would be off in regard to money matters during the ensuing two weeks.

"Tight as a drum," was answered.

"I'm sorry to hear that," replied Ellis, showing more disappointment than he wished to appear; "for I have made some calculation on you. I have nearly two thousand dollars to take care of in the next ten days."

"I wish I could help you. But, indeed, I can not," said Wilkinson, looking serious. "I have been a good deal crowded of late, and shall have my hands full, and more than full for some time to come. I never knew money so tight as it is just now."

"Nor I neither. Well, I suppose we shall get through somehow. But I must own that things look dark."

"The darkest hour is just before the break of day," said Wilkinson, with an earnestness that expressed his faith in what he said. His faith was born of a resolution to separate himself from all dangerous companionship and habits, and a deeply felt conviction of the all-sustaining strength of his wife's self-denying affection.

"Yes - yes - so the proverb says, and so the poet sings," returned Ellis, thoughtfully. "This seems to be my darkest hour. God grant it be only the precursor of day!"

"Amen!" The solemn response of Wilkinson was involuntary.

"And so you can't help me?" said Ellis, recovering himself, and speaking in a more cheerful voice.

"Indeed I cannot."

"Well, help will come, I suppose. There is nothing like trying. So good morning. Time is too precious to waste just now."

Between the store of Wilkinson and that of Ellis was a refectory, where the latter often repaired for a lunch and something to drink about eleven or twelve o'clock. It was now twelve, and, as Ellis had taken only a light breakfast, and omitted his morning dram, he felt both hungry and dry. Almost as a matter of course, he was about entering this drinking-house, when, as he

T. S. Arthur

stepped on the threshold, his eyes rested on the form of Carlton, standing by the bar with a glass in his hand. Quickly he turned away, and kept on to his store, where he quenched his thirst with a copious draught of ice-water. Not a drop of liquor had passed his lips when he went home at dinner-time. And he was as free from its influence when he joined his family at the close of day. Cara received him with the kindness and consideration that were so grateful to his feelings; and he spent the evening, safe from all dangers, at home.

CHAPTER XVII

"WILL you have the money now, dear?" said Mrs. Wilkinson, as she arose, with her husband, from the dinner-table, on the day she announced to him the fact that she had saved a few hundred dollars, out of the amount given her for the expenses of the family.

"No, not to-day," replied Wilkinson. "In fact, Mary," he added, "I don't feel just right about taking your money; and I think I must manage to get along without it."

"John!" Mrs. Wilkinson seemed hurt by her husband's words.

"It is yours, Mary," was replied with much tenderness of manner. "You have saved it for some particular purpose, and I shall not feel happy to let it go back again and become absorbed in my business."

"Have we divided interests, John?" said Mrs. Wilkinson, in a low, serious voice, as she clung to her husband's arm, and looked steadily into his face.

"I hope not, Mary."

"Am I not your wife?"

T. S. Arthur

"Yes, yes; and one of the best of wives."

"And do I not love you?"

"Never for a single moment has a doubt of your love been whispered in my heart."

"Such a whisper would have wronged me. Yes, my husband, I do love you, and as my very life."

Wilkinson bent down and pressed his lips to hers.

"Love ever seeks to bless its object," continued Mary, "and finds, in doing so, its purest delight. Do you think I could use the money I have, in any way that would bring me so much pleasure as by placing it in your hands? Surely your heart says no."

"I will take it, dear," said Wilkinson, after a slight pause. His voice was unsteady as he spoke; "and you will have your reward," he added, in tones filled with a prophecy for the future.

"Never - never - never shall act of mine bring a shadow to that dear face!" was the mental ejaculation of Wilkinson, as, with an impulse of affection he could not restrain, he threw his arms around his wife and hugged her to his bosom.

"Bless you! Bless you, Mary!" came, almost sobbing, from his overflowing heart.

On his way to his store, that afternoon, Wilkinson felt the old desire to stop and get his usual glass of brandy, and he was actually about to enter a drinking-house, when the image of his wife came so distinctly before his mind, that it seemed almost like a personal presence. He saw a shadow upon her face, and the dimness of tears was in her tender blue eyes.

"No!" said he resolutely, and with an audible expression, and quickly passed on.

How his bosom rose and fell, with a panting motion, as if from some strong physical effort.

"What an escape! It was the very path of danger!" such were his thoughts. "To venture into that path again were the folly of a madman. No, Mary, no! Your love shall draw me back with its strong attraction. A new light seems breaking all around me. I see as I never saw before. There is the broad way to destruction, and here winds the narrow but pleasant path of safety. Ruined hopes, broken hearts, and sad wrecks of humanity are scattered thickly along the first, but heavenly confidence, joyful hearts, and man, with the light of celestial truth upon his upturned face, is to be found in the other. Shall I hesitate in which to walk? No!"

With a quicker and more elastic step Wilkinson pursued his way, and reached his store just as a customer from the country, who had been waiting for him, was leaving.

"Just in time," said the latter. "I've been waiting for you over half an hour."

"I dined later to-day than usual," returned Wilkinson.

"I wanted to settle my bill, but there were two or three items which your clerk could not explain. So I concluded to let the matter stand over until I was in the city again, which will be in the course of a few weeks. However, as you are here, we will arrange it now."

So the two men walked back to the desk upon which lay Wilkinson's account books. The customer's bill was referred to, and one or two slight discrepancies reconciled. The amount of it was nearly two hundred dollars.

"You will take off five per cent. for cash, I presume?"

"Certainly," replied Wilkinson.

The money was paid down.

"So much for not stopping on the way to business for a glass of brandy."

This thought was spontaneous in the mind of Wilkinson. After his customer had left, he fell into a musing state, in which many thoughts were presented, that, from the pain and self-condemnation they occasioned, he tried to push from his mind. But he was not able to do this. Much of the history of his daily life for the past few years presented itself, and, in reviewing it, many things stood out in bold relief, which were before regarded as of little moment. Not until now did he clearly see the dangerous position in which he stood.

"So near the brink of ruin!" he sighed. "I knew the path to be a dangerous one; I knew that other feet had slipped; but felt secure in my own strength. Ah! that strength was weakness itself. I a drunkard!" He shuddered as the thought presented itself. "And Mary, the hopeless, brokenhearted wife of one lost to every ennobling sentiment of the human mind! It is awful to think of it!"

Wilkinson was deeply disturbed. For some time longer his mind dwelt on this theme: then, in the depths of his own thoughts, and in the presence of Heaven, he resolved to be in safety, by avoiding the path of danger; to put forever from his lips the cup from which he had so often drank confusion.

Suddenly he appeared to be lifted above the level he had occupied, into a region whose atmosphere was purer, and to a position from which he saw things in new relations. It was only then that he fully comprehended the real danger from which he had escaped.

"And my wife has saved me!" was the involuntary acknowledgment of his heart.

The rest of the afternoon was spent by Wilkinson in a careful investigation of his affairs. He ascertained the entire amount he would have to pay in the coming six months, and also his probable resources during the time. The result was very discouraging. But for the sum lost to Carlton he would have seen all clear; but the abstraction of so much lessened his available means, and would so clog the wheels of his business as to make all progress exceedingly difficult.

There was a shadow on the brow of Wilkinson when he met his wife that evening, and she saw it the moment he came in, notwithstanding his effort to seem cheerful. This shadow fell upon her heart, but she did not permit its reproduction on her countenance.

After tea, Mary was busied for a short time in getting little Ella to sleep. When she returned, at length, to their sitting-room, she had a small package in her hand, which, with a smiling face, she laid upon the table at which her husband sat reading.

"What is that, dear?" he asked, lifting his eyes to her face.

"We shall soon see," was answered, and Mrs. Wilkinson commenced opening the package. In a moment or two, five or six rolls of coin were produced, nicely enveloped in paper.

"This is my sub-treasury," said she, with a smile. "I took an account of the deposits to-day, and find just five hundred and fifty dollars. So, even if Mr. Ellis should fail to return the two hundred dollars he borrowed, you will still be three hundred and fifty dollars better off than you thought you were. So push every gloomy thought from your heart. All will come out right in the end."

Wilkinson looked at the money like one who could scarcely believe the evidence of his senses.

"This for the present," said Mrs. Wilkinson, leaning towards her husband, and fixing her gentle, yet earnest, loving eyes upon his face. "This for the present. And now let me give you my plans for the future. Your business is to earn money, and mine to expend so much of it as domestic comfort and well-being requires. Thus far I believe the expenditure has not been in a just ratio to the earnings. Speak out plainly, dear husband! and say if I am not right."

Wilkinson sat silent, gradually withdrawing his eyes from those of his wife, and letting them fall to the floor.

"Yes, I am right," said the latter, after a pause. "And such being the case, you have become pressed for money to conduct your business. A change, then, is required. We must lessen our expenses. And now listen to what I have to propose. I went this afternoon to see Mrs. Capron, and she says, that if we will furnish our own room, she will board us and a nurse for ten dollars a week."

"Board us!"

"Yes, dear. Won't it be much better for us to take boarding for two or three years, until we can afford to keep a house?"

"But our furniture, Mary? What is to be done with that?"

"All provided for," said Mrs. Wilkinson, with sparkling eyes, and a countenance flushed with the excitement she felt. "We will have a sale."

"A sale!"

"Yes, a sale. And this will give you more money. We will live at half the present cost, and you will get back into your business at least a thousand dollars that never should have been taken from it."

"But the sacrifice, Mary!" said Wilkinson, as if seeking an argument against his wife.

T. S. Arthur

"Did you never hear of such a thing," she replied, "as throwing over a part of the cargo to save the ship?"

"Bless you! Bless you, Mary!" exclaimed Wilkinson, in a broken voice, as he hid his face upon his wife's bosom. "You have, indeed, saved me from shipwreck, body and soul, just as I was about to be thrown upon the breakers! Heaven will reward your devoted love, your tenderness, your long-suffering and patient forbearance. Thank God for such a wife!"

And the whole frame of the strong man quivered.

It was many minutes before either of them spoke; then Mr. Wilkinson lifted his face, and said calmly -

"Yes, Mary, we will do as you propose; for you have spoken wisely. I will need every dollar in my business that I can get. And now let me say a few words more. In times past I have not been as kind to you - as considerate -"

"Dear husband! let the past be as if it had not been. You were always kind, gentle, loving" -

"Let me speak what is in my mind. I wish to give it utterance," interrupted Wilkinson. "In times past, I have too often sought companionship from home, and such companionship has ever been dangerous and debasing. I have this day resolved to correct that error; and I will keep my resolution. Henceforth, home shall be to me the dearest place. And there is one more thing I wish to say" -

The voice of Wilkinson changed its expression, while a slight flush came into his face.

"There is one habit that I have indulged, and which I feel to be an exceedingly dangerous one. That habit I have solemnly promised, in the sight of Heaven, to correct. I will no longer put to my lips the cup of confusion."

Wilkinson was not prepared for the effect these words had upon his wife, who, instantly uttering a cry of joy, flung herself into her husband's arms, sobbing -

"Oh! I am the happiest woman alive this day!"

T. S. Arthur

CHAPTER XVIII

TO Ellis the trials of the next two weeks were of the severest character. Yet, he kept himself away from drinking-houses, and struggled manfully to retain his feet under him. In this he was only sustained by the kindness of his wife's manner, and the interest she seemed to feel in him. Had she acted towards him with her usual want of affectionate consideration, he would have fallen under the heavy burdens that rested upon him. Scarcely a day passed in which he was not visited by Carlton's agent, and fretted almost past endurance by his importunities. But he steadily refused to take up any of the due-bills; at the same time that he promised to cancel them at some future period. This did not, of course, suit the gambler, who sent threats of an immediate resort to legal proceedings.

Of all this Cara knew nothing; yet she could not help seeing that her husband was troubled, and this caused her to muse on what she had done with increasing uneasiness. She no longer took any pleasure in the thoughts of new parlour carpets. But it was too late, now, to retrace her steps of error. The carpets were already in the hands of the upholsterers, and a few days would see them on the floor.

"I must tell him about them," said Cara to herself, about a week after her act of folly, as she sat, towards the close of day, brooding over what she had done. "To be forewarned is to be forearmed. In a few days the carpets will be sent home, and then" -

A slight inward shudder was felt by Cara, as she paused, with the sentence unfinished.

"But I'm foolish," she added, recovering herself, "very foolish. Why need I be so afraid of Henry? I have some freedom of action left - some right of choice. These were not all yielded in our marriage. His will was not made the imperative law of all my actions. No - no. And here lies the ground of difference between us. The fact is, he is to blame for this very thing, for he drove me to it."

But such thoughts did not satisfy the mind of Mrs. Ellis, nor remove the sense of wrong that oppressed her spirit. So, in a little while, she came back to her resolution to tell her husband, on that very evening, all about what she had done. This was her state of mind, when her friend Mrs. Claxton called in. After the first pleasant greeting, the lady, assuming a slight gravity of manner, said -

"Do you know, Mrs. Ellis, that I've thought a good deal about the matter we talked of the last time I saw you?"

"To what do you allude?" asked Cara.

"To running up bills without your husband's knowledge. All men are not alike, and Mr. Ellis might not take it so easily as Mr. Claxton has done. The fact is, I have been checked off a little, so to speak, within a day or two, and it has rather set me to thinking"

T. S. Arthur

"In what way?" inquired Mrs. Ellis.

"I will tell you - but, remember, this is in the strictest confidence. It might injure my husband's business if it got out. In fact, I don't think I have any right to tell you; but, as I advised you to follow my example, I must give you convincing proof that this example is a bad one. Last evening, when Mr. Claxton came home, he looked unusually serious. 'Is any thing wrong?' I asked of him, manifesting in my voice and manner the concern I really felt. 'Yes,' said he, looking me fixedly in the eyes - 'there is something wrong. I came within an ace of being protested to-day.' 'Indeed! How?' I exclaimed. 'Listen,' said he, 'and you shall hear; and while you hear, believe, for I solemnly declare that every word I utter is the truth, and nothing but the truth. I could not spare the cash when your new carpet and upholstery bill came in, so I gave a note for the amount, which was over two hundred dollars. The note was for six months, and fell due to-day. I also gave a note for your new sofa, chairs, and French bedstead, because I had no cash with which to pay the bill. It was two hundred and fifty dollars, and the note given at four months. That also fell due to-day. Now, apart from these, I had more than my hands full to take up business paper, this being an unusually heavy day. At every point where I could do so I borrowed; but at half-past two o'clock I was still short the amount of these two notes. While in the utmost doubt and perplexity as to what I should do in my difficulty, two notes were handed in. One contained a dry goods bill which you had run up of over a hundred and fifty dollars, and the other a shoe bill of twenty-five. I cannot describe to you the paralyzing sense of discouragement that instantly came over me. It is hopeless for me to struggle on at such a disadvantage, said I to myself - utterly hopeless. And I determined to give up the struggle - to let my notes lie over, and thus end the unequal strife in which I was engaged; for, to this, I saw it must come at last. Full twenty minutes went by, and I still sat in this state of irresolution. Then, as a vivid perception of consequences came to my mind, I aroused myself to make a last, desperate effort. Hurriedly drawing a note at thirty days for five hundred dollars, I took it to a money-lender, whom I knew I could tempt by the offer of a large discount. He gave me for it a check on the bank in which my notes were deposited, for four hundred and fifty dollars. Just as the clock was striking three, I entered the banking-house.'

"My husband paused. I saw by the workings of his face and by the large beads of perspiration which stood upon his forehead, that he was indeed in earnest. I never was so startled by any thing in my life. It seemed for a time as if it were only a dream. I need not say how sincerely I repented of what I had done, nor how I earnestly promised my husband never again to contract a debt of even a dollar without his knowledge. I hope," added Mrs. Claxton, "that you have not yet been influenced by my advice and example; and I come thus early to speak in your ears a word of caution. Pray do not breathe aught of what I have told you - it might injure my husband - I only make the revelation as a matter of duty to one I tried to lead astray."

The thoughts of Mrs. Ellis did not run in a more peaceful channel after the departure of her friend. But she resolved to confess every thing to her husband, and promise to conform herself more to his wishes in the future.

"What," she said, "if he should be in like business difficulties with Mr. Claxton? He has looked serious for a week past, and has remained at home every evening during the time - a thing unusual. And I don't think he has used liquor as freely as common. Something is the matter. Oh, I wish I had not done that!"

While such thoughts were passing through the mind of Mrs. Ellis, her husband came home. She met him with an affectionate manner, which he returned. But there was a cloud on his brow that even her smile could not drive away. Even as she met him, words of confession were on the tongue of Mrs. Ellis, but she shrank from giving them utterance.

After tea she resolved to speak. But, when this set-time of acknowledgment came, she was as little prepared for the task as before. Mr. Ellis looked so troubled, that she could not find it in her heart to add to the pressure on his mind an additional weight. And so the evening passed, the secret of Mrs. Ellis remaining undivulged. And so, day after day went on.

At length, one morning, the new carpet was sent home and put down. It was a beautiful carpet; but, as Mrs. Ellis stood looking upon it, after the upholsterer had departed, she found none of the pleasure she anticipated.

"Oh, why, why, why did I do this?" she murmured. "Why was I tempted to such an act of folly?"

Gradually the new carpet faded from the eyes of Mrs. Ellis, and she saw only the troubled face of her husband. It was within an hour of dinner-time, and in painful suspense she waited his arrival. Various plans for subduing the excitement which she saw would be created in his mind, and for reconciling him to the expense of the carpets, were thought over by Mrs. Ellis: among those was a proposition that he should give a note for the bill, which she would pay, when it matured, out of savings from her weekly allowance of money.

"I can and will do it," said Mrs. Ellis, resolutely: her thought dwelt longer and longer on this suggestion. "I hope he will not be too angry to listen to what I have to say, when he comes home and sees the carpet. He's rather hasty sometimes."

While in the midst of such thoughts, Mrs. Ellis, who had left the parlour, heard the shutting of the street-door, and the tread of her husband in the passage. Glancing at the timepiece on the mantel, she saw that it was half an hour earlier than he usually came home. Eagerly she bent her ear to listen. All was soon still. He had entered the rooms below, or paused on the threshold. A few breathless moments passed, then a smothered exclamation was heard, followed by two or three heavy foot-falls and the jarring of the outer door. Mr. Ellis had left the house!

"Gone! What does it mean?" exclaimed Mrs. Ellis, striking her hands together, while a strange uneasiness fell upon her heart. A long time she sat listening for sounds of his return; but she waited in vain. It was fully an hour past their usual time for dining, when she sat down to the table with her children, but not to partake of food herself. Leaving Mrs. Ellis to pass the remainder of that unhappy day with her own troubled and upbraiding thoughts, we will return to her husband, and see how it fares with him.

CHAPTER XIX

FOR hours after his wife had sunk into the forgetfulness of sleep, Ellis lay awake, pondering over the ways and means by which he was to meet his engagements for the next day, which, exclusive of Carlton's demand, were in the neighbourhood of a thousand dollars. During the previous two weeks, he had paid a good deal of money, but he was really but little better off therefor, the money so paid having been mainly procured through temporary loans from business friends. Most of it he had promised to return on the morrow. Earnestly as the mind of Ellis dwelt on the subject, he was not able to devise the means of getting safely through the next day.

"And what if I do get over the difficult place?" was the desponding conclusion of his mind - "ultimate failure is inevitable, unless a great reduction can be made in expenses. At present, our living exceeds the profits on my business. Ah! if I could only make Cara understand this! She has been more considerate and wife-like of late; but I fear to say one word about the embarrassed state of my affairs, lest the sunshine of love be again darkened with clouds and storms."

With such thoughts in his mind, Ellis fell asleep.

On the next morning, he repaired early to his place of

business, in order to have time fully to digest his plan of operations for the day. He had many doubts as to his ability to get through, but was resolute not to yield without a vigorous struggle. Of the amount to be paid, only four hundred was for notes in bank. The rest was on borrowed money account. Fully an hour and a half was spent in drawing off certain accounts, and in determining the line of operations for the morning. On receiving two hundred dollars for these accounts, Ellis thought he might with safety calculate; and a lad was sent out to see to their collection. Then he started forth himself. First in order, he deemed it best to see if he could not get a little more time on some of his borrowed money. This was a delicate operation, and its attempt could only, he felt, be justified by the exigencies of the case. The largest sum to be returned was three hundred dollars. He had borrowed it from a merchant in good circumstances, who could at any time command his thousands, and to whose credit there usually remained heavy balances in bank. But he was exceedingly punctilious in all business matters.

Both these facts Ellis knew. It would put the merchant to no inconvenience whatever to continue the accommodation for ten days longer; but the policy of asking this was felt to be a very questionable one, as it would be most likely to create in his mind a doubt of Ellis's standing, and a doubt in that quarter would be injurious. Still, the case was so pressing, that Ellis determined to see him. So, assuming a pleasant, partly unconcerned air, he called upon the merchant.

"Good morning, Mr. A -," said he, in a cheerful tone.

"Good morning, friend Ellis," returned the merchant, pushing his spectacles above his forehead, and fixing

T. S. Arthur

his eyes upon the face of his visitor, with a sharp, penetrating look which rather belied the smile that played about his lips.

"Let me see! Isn't it to-day that I am to return you the three hundred dollars borrowed last week?"

"I don't remember, but can tell you in a moment," replied A -,replacing his glasses, and taking from a pigeon-hole in the desk before which he sat a small memorandum-book. After consulting this, he replied -

"Yes: you are right. It is to be returned to-day."

"So I thought. Very well. I'll send you a check around during the morning. That will answer, I presume?"

"Oh, certainly - certainly."

So far, nothing was gained. A hurried debate, as to the policy of asking a few days more on the loan, took place in the mind of Ellis. He then said -

"If just the same to you, it will be more convenient for me to return this money on the day after to-morrow."

There was a slight contraction of brow on the part of Mr. A -, who replied, rather coldly -

"I shall want it to-day, Mr. Ellis."

"Oh, very well - very well," said Ellis, hiding artfully his disappointment. "It will be all the same. I will send you around a check in a little while."

As he left the store, A - said to himself -

"Of all things, I like to see punctuality in the matter of engagements. The man who promises to return in an hour the money he borrows from you should keep his word to the minute."

The failure to get a few days' extension of time on so important a sum had the effect to dispirit Ellis a good deal. He left the store of the merchant in a despondent mood, and was returning towards his own place of business, when he met Wilkinson. Grasping the hand of the latter with the eagerness of one who knows, in a great extremity, that he is face to face with a real friend, he said -

"You must help me to-day."

"I don't see that it is possible, Ellis," was replied. "What amount do you want?"

"I must have a thousand dollars."

"So much?"

"Yes. But where the sum is to be obtained is more than I can divine."

"Is all to go into bank?"

"No. Six hundred is for borrowed money."

"To whom is the latter due?"

"I must return three hundred to A -."

"He can do without it for a few days longer."

T. S. Arthur

"I have just seen him; but he says it must be returned to-day."

"He does?"

"Yes. He wants to use it."

Wilkinson stood thoughtfully for some time.

"Can you return the sum in a week?" he then asked.

"O yes; easily."

"Very well I'll go and ask him to loan me three hundred for a week. He'll do it, I know. You shall have the use of it for the time specified."

"If you can get me that sum, you will place me under an everlasting obligation," said Ellis, with more feeling than he wished to display.

Twenty minutes afterward the money was in his hands. It had been obtained from A -, and during the morning returned to him in payment of Ellis's loan.

So much accomplished, Ellis turned his thoughts towards the ways and means for raising the seven hundred dollars yet required for the day's business. By twelve o'clock all of his borrowed money was returned; but his notes still remained in bank. In view of the difficulties yet to be surmounted, he felt that he had erred in not making it the first business of the day to take up his notes, and thus get beyond the danger of protest. But it was too late now for regrets to be of any avail. Four hundred dollars must come from some quarter, or ruin was certain.

But from whence was aid to come? He had not spent an idle moment since he came to his store in the morning, and had so fully passed over the limits within which his resources lay, that little ground yet remained to be broken, and the promise of that was small.

While Ellis stood meditating, in much perplexity of mind, what step next to take, a man entered his store, and, approaching him, read aloud from a paper which he drew from his pocket, a summons to answer before an alderman in the case of Carlton, who had brought separate suits on his due-bills, each being for an amount less than one hundred dollars.

"Very well, I will attend to it," said Ellis in a voice of assumed calmness, and the officer retired.

Slowly seating himself in a chair that stood by a low writing-desk, the unhappy man tried to compose his thoughts, in order that he might see precisely in what position this new move would place him. He could bring nothing in bar of Carlton's claim unless the plea of its being a gambling debt were urged; and that would only ruin his credit in the business community. A hearing of the case was to take place in a week, when judgment would go against him, and then the quick work of an execution would render the imme- diate payment of the five hundred dollars necessary. All this Ellis revolved in his thoughts, and then deliberately asked himself the question, if it were not better to give up at once. For a brief space of time, in the exhausted state produced by the un-equal struggle in which he was engaged, he felt like abandoning every thing; but a too-vivid realization of the consequences that would inevitably follow spurred his mind into a resolution to make one more vigorous effort to overcome the remaining difficulties of the day. With this new purpose, came a new suggestion of means, and he was in the act of leaving his store to call upon a friend not before thought of, when a carpet dealer, whom he knew very well, came in, and presented a bill.

"What is this?" asked Mr. Ellis.

"The bill for your parlour carpets," was answered.

"What parlour carpets? You are in an error. We have no new parlour carpets. The bill is meant for some one else."

"Oh, no," returned the man, smiling. "The carpets were ordered two weeks ago; and this morning they were put down by the upholsterer."

"Who ordered them?"

"Mrs. Ellis."

"She did!"

"Yes; and directed the bill sent in to you?"

"What is the amount?"

"One hundred and sixty-eight dollars."

"Very well," said Ellis, controlling himself, "I will attend to it."

The man retired, leaving the mind of Ellis in a complete sea of agitation.

"If this be so," he muttered in a low, angry voice, "then is all over! To struggle against such odds is hopeless. But I cannot believe it. There is - there must be an error. The carpets are not mine. He has mistaken some other woman for my wife, and some other dwelling for mine. Yes, yes, it must be so. Cara would never dare to do this! But all doubt may be quickly settled."

And with, this last sentence on his lips, Ellis left his store, and walked with hurried steps homeward. Entering his house, he stood for a moment or two in one of the parlour doors. A single glance sufficed. Alas! it was but too true.

"Mad woman!" he exclaimed, in a low, bitter tone. "Mad woman! You have driven me over the precipice!"

Turning quickly away, he left the house - to return to his store? - Alas! no. With him the struggle was over. The manly spirit, that had, for nearly two weeks, battled so bravely with difficulty without and temptation within, yielded under this last assault. In less than an hour, all sense of pain was lost in the stupor of inebriation!

T. S. Arthur

CHAPTER XX

WE will not trace, minutely, the particulars attendant on the headlong downward course of Henry Ellis. The causes leading thereto have been fully set forth, and we need not refer back to them. Enough, that the fall was complete. The wretched man appeared to lose all strength of mind, all hope in life, all self-respect. Not even a feeble effort was opposed to the down-rushing torrent of disaster that swept away every vestige of his business. For more than a week he kept himself so stupefied with brandy, that neither friends nor creditors could get from him any intelligible statement in regard to his affairs. In the wish of the latter for an assignment, he passively acquiesced, and permitted all his effects to be taken from his hands. And so he was thrown upon the world, with his family, helpless, penniless, crushed in spirit, and weak as a child in the strong grasp of an over-mastering appetite, which had long been gathering strength for his day of weakness.

Over the sad history of the succeeding five years let us draw a veil. We have no heart to picture its suffering, its desolation, its hopelessness. If, in the beginning, there was too much pride in the heart of Mrs. Ellis, all was crushed out under the iron heel of grim adversity. If she had once thought too much of herself, and too little of her husband, a great change succeeded; for she clung to him in all the cruel and disgusting forms his abandonment assumed, and, with a self-sacrificing devotion, struggled with the fearful odds against her to retain for her husband and children some little warmth in the humble home where they were hidden from the world in which they once moved.

From the drunkard, angels withdraw themselves, and evil spirits come into nearer companionship; hence, the bestiality and cruelty of drunkenness. The man, changing his internal associates, receives by inflex a new order of influence, and passively acts therefrom. He becomes, for the time, the human agent by which evil spirits effect their wicked purposes; and it usually happens that those who are nearest allied to him, and who have the first claims on him for support, protection, and love, are they who feel the heaviest weight of infernal malice. The husband and father too often becomes, in the hands of his evil associates, the cruel persecutor of those he should love and guard with the tenderest solicitude. So it was in the case of Henry Ellis. His manly nature underwent a gradually progressing change, until the image of God was wellnigh obliterated from his soul. After the lapse of five miserable years, let us introduce him and his family once more to the reader.

Five years! What a work has been done in that time! Not in a pleasant home, surrounded with every comfort, as we last saw them, will they be found. Alas, no!

It was late in the year. Frost had already done its work upon the embrowned forests, and leaf by leaf the withered foliage had dropped away or been swept in clouds before the autumnal winds. Feebler and feebler grew, daily, the sun's planting rays, colder the air, and more cheerless the aspect of nature.

One evening, - it was late in November, and the day had been damp and cold, - a woman, whose thin care-worn face and slender form marked her as an invalid, or one whose spirits had been broken by trouble, was busying herself in the preparation of supper. A girl, between twelve and thirteen years of age, was trying to amuse a child two years old, who, from some cause, was in a fretful humour; and a little girl in her seventh year was occupied with a book, in which she was spelling out a lesson that had been given by her mother. This was the family, or, rather, a part of the family of Henry Ellis. Two members were absent, the father and the oldest boy. The room was small, and meagerly furnished, though every thing was clean and in order. In the centre of the floor, extending, perhaps, over half thereof, was a piece of faded carpet. On this a square, unpainted pine table stood, covered with a clean cloth and a few dishes. Six common wooden chairs, one or two low stools or benches, a stained work-stand without drawers, and a few other necessary articles, including a bed in one corner, completed the furniture of this apartment, which was used as kitchen and sitting-room by the family, and, with a small room adjoining, constituted the entire household facilities of the family.

"Henry is late this evening," remarked Mrs. Ellis, as she laid the last piece of toast she had been making on the dish standing near the fire. "He ought to have been here half an hour ago."

"And father is late too," said Kate, the oldest daughter, who was engaged with the fretful child.

"Yes - he is late," returned Mrs. Ellis, as if speaking to herself. And she sighed heavily.

Just then the sound of feet was heard in the passage without.

"There's Henry now," said Kate.

And in a moment after the boy entered. His face did not wear the cheerful expression with which he usually met the waiting ones at home. His mother noticed the change; but asked no question then as to the cause.

"I wish father was home," said Mrs. Ellis. "Supper is all ready."

"I don't think it's any use to wait for him," returned Henry.

"Why not?" asked the mother, looking with some surprise at her son, in whose voice was a covert meaning.

"Because he won't be home to supper."

"Have you seen him, Henry?"

Mrs. Ellis fixed her eyes earnestly upon her son.

"Yes, mother. I saw him go into a tavern as I was coming along. I went in and tried to persuade him to come home with me. But he was angry about something, and told me to go about my business. I then said - 'Do, father, come home with me,' and took hold of his arm, when he turned quickly around, and slapped me in the face with the back of his hand."

T. S. Arthur

The boy, on saying this, burst into tears, and sobbed for some time violently.

"Oh, Henry! did he do that?"

Such was the mother's exclamation. She tried to control her feelings, but could not. In a moment or two, tears gushed over her face.

The only one who appeared calm was Kate, Henry's oldest sister. She uttered no expression of pain or surprise, but, after hearing what her brother said, looked down upon the floor, and seemed lost in meditation.

"My poor children!" such were the thoughts that passed through the mind of Mrs. Ellis. "If I could only screen you from these dreadful consequences! If I only were the sufferer, I could bear the burden uncomplainingly. Ah! will this cup never be full? Is there no hope? How earnestly I have sought to win him back again, Heaven only knows."

From these reflections Mrs. Ellis was aroused by the voice of Kate, who had arisen up and was taking from a nail in the wall her bonnet and an old merino coat.

"Where is the tavern, Henry?" said she.

"What tavern?" answered the boy.

"The tavern where you saw father."

"In Second street."

"Why do you wish to know?" inquired Mrs. Ellis.

"I will go for him. He'll come home for me."

"No - no, Kate. Don't think of such a thing!" said Mrs. Ellis, speaking from the impulse of the moment.

"It won't be of any use," remarked Henry. "Besides, it's very dark out, sister, and the tavern where I saw him is a long distance from here. Indeed I wouldn't go, Kate. He isn't at all himself."

The young girl was not in the least influenced by this opposition, but, rather, strengthened in her purpose. She knew that the air was damp and chilly, from an approaching easterly storm; and the thought of his being exposed to cold and rain at night, in the streets, touched her heart with a painful interest in her erring, debased, and fallen parent.

"It will rain to-night," said she, looking at her brother.

"I felt a fine mist in the driving wind just as I came near the door," replied Henry.

"If father is not himself, he may fall in the street, and perish in the cold."

"I don't think there is any danger of that, sister. He will be home after awhile. At any rate, there is little chance of your finding him, for he won't be likely to remain long at the tavern where I left him."

"If I can't find him, so much the worse," replied the girl, firmly. "But, unless mother forbids my going, I must seek him and bring him home."

Kate turned her eyes full upon her mother's face, as she

said this, and, in an attitude of submission, awaited her reply.

"I think," said Mrs. Ellis, after a long silence, "that little good will come of this; yet, I cannot say no."

"Then I will find him and bring him home," was the animated response of Kate.

"You must not go alone," remarked Henry, taking up the cap he had a few minutes before laid off.

"Wait for supper. It is all ready," said Mrs. Ellis. "Don't go out until you have eaten something."

"No time is to be lost, mother," replied Kate. "And, then, I haven't the least appetite."

"But your brother has been working hard all day, and is, of course, tired and hungry."

"Oh, I forgot," said Kate. "But Henry needn't go with me. If he will only tell me exactly where I can find father, that will be enough. I think I'd better see him alone."

"Food would choke me now." Henry's voice was husky and tremulous. "Come, sister," he added, after a pause, "if this work is done at all, it must be done quickly."

Without a word more on either part, the brother and sister left the room, and started on their errand.

CHAPTER XXI

LATE in the afternoon of the day on which occurred the incidents mentioned in the preceding chapter, Mr. Wilkinson, who had entirely recovered from his embarrassed condition, and who was now a sober man in every sense of the word, as well as a thrifty merchant, was standing at one of the counters in his large, well filled store, when a miserable looking creature entered and came back to where he stood.

"Good-day, Mr. Wilkinson," said the new-comer.

Surprise kept the merchant silent for some moments, when the other said -

"You don't know me, I presume."

"Henry Ellis!" exclaimed Wilkinson. "Is it possible you have fallen so low?"

"Just as you see me," was replied.

"You ought to be more of a man than this. You ought to have more strength of character," said Wilkinson, giving utterance to the first thought that came into his mind.

"Oh, yes; it is easy to talk," replied Ellis, with a slight

impatience of manner. "But you know my history as well almost as I know it myself. I was driven to ruin."

"How so?"

"Why do you ask the question?"

"You refer to your wife?"

"Of course I do. She drove me to destruction."

"That is a hard saying, Mr. Ellis."

"Yet true as that the sun shines. And she has had her reward!"

This last sentence was uttered in a tone of self-satisfaction that deeply pained Mr. Wilkinson.

"I saw your wife this morning," he remarked, after a moment's silence.

"You did! Where?"

"I passed her in the street; and the sight of her made my heart ache. Ah, my friend! if you have been wronged, deeply is the wrong repaid! Such a wreck! I could scarcely believe my eyes. Ellis! I read at a single glance her countenance, marred by long suffering, and found in it only the sad evidences of patient endurance. She is changed. I am bold to say that. If she erred, she has repented."

"But not atoned for a wrong that is irreparable," said Ellis in a dogged tone, while his heavy brows contracted.

"Ah! how changed you are, Ellis: once so kind-hearted, so forgiving and forbearing!"

"And what changed me? Answer me that, John Wilkinson! Yes, I am changed - changed from a man into - into - yes, let me say the word - into a devil! And who held the enchanter's wand? Who? The wife of my bosom!"

Wilkinson felt a shudder creeping along his nerves as he looked at the excited man, and heard his words.

"Cara never acts toward you, now, other than with kindness," said he.

But Ellis made no answer to this.

"Let the past suffice, my friend," added Wilkinson. "Both have suffered enough. Resolve, in the strength of God and your own manhood, to rise out of the horrible pit and miry clay into which you have fallen."

"That is impossible. So we won't talk about it," said Ellis, impatiently. "Lend me half a dollar, won't you?"

The hand of Wilkinson went instinctively to his pocket. But he withdrew it, without the coin he had designed, from the moment's impulse, to give. Shaking his head, he replied to the application,

"I can't give you money, Ellis."

"You can't?"

"No; for that would be no real kindness. But, if you will reform your life; if you will abandon drink, and

T. S. Arthur

become a sober, industrious man, I will pledge myself to procure you a good situation as clerk. In a few years you may regain all that has been lost."

"Bah!" muttered Ellis, grinding his teeth as he spoke. "All good talk!" and, turning away, he passed from the store of his old friend. Without a cent in his pocket, and burning with a desire for drink, he had conquered all reluctance and shame, and applied, as we have seen, to an old friend, for money. Two or three other ineffectual attempts were made to get small sums, but they proved fruitless. For some time he wandered about the streets; then he entered one of the lower class of taverns, and boldly called for a glass of liquor. But the keeper of this den, grown suspicious by experience, saw in the face or manner of Ellis that he had no money, and coolly demanded pay before setting forth his bottle. It was just at this untimely crisis that Henry came in, and, taking hold of his father's arm, urged him to come home. The cruel rebuff he received is known.

The blow was no sooner given by Ellis than repented of; and this motion of regret prompted him to express his sorrow for the hasty act, but when he turned to speak to the lad, he was gone. Almost maddened by thirst and excitement, the poor wretch caught up from the counter a pitcher of ice water, and, placing it to his lips, took therefrom a long deep draught. Then slowly turning away, he sought a chair in a far corner of the room; where he seated himself, crossed his arms on a table, and buried his face therein.

The pure cold water allayed the fever that burned along the drunkard's veins. Gradually a deep calm pervaded his mind, and then thought became active amid thronging memories of the past. He had once loved his home and his children; and the image of Henry, when a bright-eyed, curly-headed, happy child, came up so vividly before him, that it was only by an effort that he kept the tears from gushing over his face. For years he had cherished, in mere self-justification, the bitterest feeling towards his wife; and hundreds of times had he given expression to these feelings in words that smote the heart of Cara with crushing force. Only a little while before he had spoken of her, in the presence of Wilkinson, in a hard and unforgiving spirit; but now he thought of her more kindly. He remembered how patiently she had borne with him; how uncomplainingly she had met and struggled with her hard lot; how many times she had tried to smile upon him, even through tears that could not be restrained. Never was he met, on his return home, with coldness or neglect. Wife and children all sought his comfort; yet he cared nothing for them, and even filled their paths through life with thorns. And his boy, Henry, whom he had just repulsed in so cruel a manner, to his labour was he indebted, mainly, for the food that was daily set before him. How this thought smote him! How it filled his heart with shame and repentance!

Musing thus, the unhappy man remained, until, gradually, his thoughts became confused. The temporary excitement of feeling died away, and sleep overcame him. In his sleep he dreamed, and his dream was vivid as reality. Not as of old did he find himself; but, in the vision that came to him, he was still in bondage and degradation, with a horribly distinct realization of his condition. His vile companions were around him, but greatly changed; for they appeared more like monsters of evil than men, and were malignant in their efforts to do harm. Against him they seemed to feel an especial hatred. Some glared and

T. S. Arthur

gleamed upon him with the fire of murder in their eyes; some pointed to a cheerless apartment, in which he saw his wife and children cowering and shivering over a few dying embers, and they said - "It is your work! It is your work!" They were devils in distorted human shapes, and he was terribly afraid. Suddenly he was set upon by one, who caught him by the throat and dragged him into what seemed the cell of a prison, where he was cast upon a heap of straw, and left shuddering with cold and fear. Alone, for days and weeks he remained in this prison, until despair seemed to dry up the very blood in his veins, and, after a desperate struggle to break through the bars of his narrow house, he sank down exhausted and ready to die. Then came a new horror. He had died, to all outward appearance, and was in his coffin. He felt his body compressed, and gasped and panted for air in his narrow house of boards. It was an awful moment. Suddenly a voice came to his ear: "Father! father!" It was the voice of his child - of Kate. How its tones thrilled through him! How his heart leaped with the hope of deliverance! "Father! dear father!" - The call was renewed, but he could make no answer, for his tongue was powerless. Again and again the call was repeated, yet he could utter no sound - could make no sign. Farther off, then, he heard his name called. Horror! she had failed to discover him, and was about departing. In the agony of the moment he awoke. There was a hand laid gently upon him, and a voice said - "Father! dear father! come!"

It was the voice of his child; the same voice that had penetrated his dreaming ear.

"Oh, Kate!" he exclaimed, eagerly; "is it indeed you?"

"Yes, father," she answered; "and won't you come home with me?"

The wretched man did not answer in words but arose immediately and went out with his daughter.

"Oh, what a dream I had, Kate!" said Mr. Ellis, as he left the door of the tavern; "and you came to me in my dream."

His feelings were much excited, and he spoke with emotion.

"Did I, father?" replied the girl. "And how did I come? As a good angel to save you?"

"Waking, you have come to me as such," answered the father after a brief silence, speaking more calmly, and as if to himself.

How wild a thrill shot through the frame of Kate at these words, so full of meaning to her; but she dared not trust herself to make an answer, lest she should do harm rather than good. And so they walked, in silence, all the way home; Henry, who had accompanied his sister, keeping a short distance behind them, so that his father had no indication of his presence.

CHAPTER XXII

How the hearts of the mother and her two oldest children trembled with hope and fear! A marked change was apparent in Mr. Ellis when he came home with Kate. He was sober, and very serious, but said nothing; and Mrs. Ellis deemed it prudent to say nothing to him.

On the next morning, he did not rise early. Henry had eaten his breakfast and was away to his work, and Kate had gone to market to get something for dinner, when he got up and dressed himself. Mrs. Ellis was ready for him with a good cup of coffee, a piece of hot toast, some broiled steak, and a couple of eggs. She said little, but her tones were subdued and very kind. Noticing that his hand trembled so that he spilled his coffee in raising his cup to his lips, (his custom was to get a glass of liquor before breakfast to steady his nerves,) she came and stood beside him, saying, as she did so - "Let me hold your cup for you."

Ellis acquiesced; and so his wife held the cup to his lips while he drank.

"Oh, dear! This is a dreadful state to be in Cara!"

The exclamation was spontaneous. Had Ellis thought a moment, his pride would have caused him to repress it.

Mrs. Ellis did not reply, for she was afraid to trust herself to speak, lest her words or voice should express something that would check the better feelings that were in the heart of her husband. But, ere she could repress it, a tear fell upon his hand. Almost with a start, Ellis turned and looked up into her face. It was calm, yet sorrowful. The pale and wasted condition of that face had never so struck him before.

"Ah, Cara," said he, dropping his knife and fork, "it is dreadful to live in this way. Dreadful! dreadful!"

The poor, almost heart-broken wife could command herself no longer; and she laid her face down upon her husband and sobbed - the more convulsively from her efforts to regain self-possession.

"Oh, Henry!" she at length murmured, "if the past were only ours! If we could but live over our lives, with some of the experience that living gives, how differently should we act! But, surely, hope is not clean gone for ever! Is there not yet a better and a brighter day for even us?"

"There is, Cara! There is!" replied Ellis, in tones of confidence. "It has been a long, long night, Cara; a cold and cheerless night. But the morning breaks. There is not much strength left in this poor arm," and he extended his right hand, that trembled like an aspen leaf - "but it can yet do something. It shall not be with us as it has been any longer. In the sight of Heaven, and in the hope of strength from above, I promise that, Cara. Will you help me to keep my promise?"

"Yes - yes - yes," was the emphatic response. "If there is in me a particle of strength, it is yours, and you may

T. S. Arthur

lean on it confidently. Oh, Henry! trust in me. The lessons of the past have not been learned in vain."

"I am very weak, Cara; the pressure of a child's hand might throw me over. Do not forget this. Never forget it! If you will keep close to my side, if you will help me, and love me," - his voice quivered, and he paused, but regained himself in a few moments - "I think all will be well with us again. God helping me, I will try."

"Oh, my husband!" sobbed Mrs. Ellis, drawing her arms lovingly about him - "it will be well with us, for God will help you, I will help you, all will help you. Forget? Oh, no! I can never forget. Have we not all been thoughtful of you, and kind to you in the night that is passing away?"

"Yes, Cara, yes."

"And will we not be kinder and more loving in the brighter future? We will! we will, Henry! Oh! how my glad heart runs over!"

"I saw Mr. Wilkinson yesterday," said Ellis, after both had grown calmer; "and he said that he could and would get me a situation as clerk. I am now going to see him, and, if he be as good as his word, this desert place" - and he glanced about the room - "will soon brighten as the rose."

The entrance of Kate closed the interview. In a little while, Ellis, after shaving himself, and in every possible way improving his appearance, left the house and went direct to the store of Wilkinson.

"Henry! Is it possible!" exclaimed the latter, in

surprise, when Ellis stood before him.

"In my right mind again," was the calm, but firmly spoken answer.

"How glad I am to hear you say so!" And Wilkinson grasped the hand of his old friend, and shook it warmly.

"You remember your promise of yesterday?" said Ellis. He spoke seriously.

"To get you a good situation?"

"Yes."

"I have not forgotten my word, Henry; and will keep it. You are a good accountant?"

"I am."

"This morning my book-keeper notified me of his intention to leave as soon as I could supply his place. If you will take the situation at seven hundred and fifty dollars a year, it is open for you."

"John Wilkinson!" exclaimed Ellis, seizing the hand of his friend, and exhibiting much agitation. "Are you indeed in earnest?"

"I never was more so in my life," was replied.

"Then, indeed the day has broken!" said Ellis, with emotion. "When will you want me to begin?" he asked after a short period of silence.

"Now," replied Wilkinson.

"Now, did you say?"

"Yes. I have work that needs attention at once. When will you come?"

"A good beginning never can be made too early. Now."

Wilkinson turned, and the two men walked back to a vacant desk. A number of accounts and letters lay thereon, and, as Wilkinson began to enter into some explanation in regard to them, Ellis took up a pen and laid the point of it on a sheet of paper. The nervous tremor of his hand showed him to be in no condition for the task upon which he was about entering. Wilkinson comprehended this in a moment, and a fear lest the drunkard's delirium should follow so sudden a withdrawal of stimulant from the system of Ellis, sent a chill through his feelings. Instead of putting him to the desk at once, he determined, on the instant, to employ him at more active work about the store for a few weeks, until, if he kept to his good resolution, some degree of firmness was restored to his shattered nerves. In agreement with this humane purpose he acted.

With what trembling anxiety did Mrs. Ellis await the return of her husband at dinner-time! The hours wore slowly away, and, at last, her watchful ear caught the sound of his footsteps. She scarcely breathed until the door opened. One glance sufficed. All was well. How glad was the impulse with which her stilled heart went on again! Tears of joy bedewed her face, when he related the good fortune that had attended his call on Wilkinson.

"Yes, yes," said he, when he had told her all, and glancing around the room as he spoke. "This desert place shall blossom as the rose. I have said it, and I will keep my word."

In the evening, Henry and his father met, for the first time, face to face, since they parted in anger on one side and grief on the other. When Kate came home with the latter on the night previous, Henry had managed to enter the house before them, and so kept out of his father's way. Now, on coming in from his work, he found him already at home, and so changed in appearance, that he gazed upon him with a surprise which he could not at first conceal.

"Henry, my son," said Mr. Ellis, in a kind, self-possessed tone of voice, and he reached out his hand as he spoke.

The boy took his father's hand, and looked earnestly into his face.

"Henry, how long have you been with Mr. Wilson?" inquired Mr. Ellis.

"Two years, sir," was answered.

The father looked at the boy's hands, and sighed. They were hard and discolored from labour.

"Tell Mr. Wilson, in the morning," said he, "that I wish you to leave him after this week."

"Sir!" Henry looked surprised.

"Tell him that I wish you to go to school for a year or two."

"Father!" The blood flew suddenly to the lad's face. For a few moments he looked at his father; then turning, he passed quickly into the adjoining room. In the stillness that followed, were audible the sobs that came from his overflowing heart.

A week, a month, a year have passed, yet the promise of that happy time is dimmed not by a single cloud. Firm in his better purpose and fully sustained at home, Henry Ellis is walking steadily the path of safety. Home is what it ever should have been, the pleasantest place in all the world; for she who is its sunlight never meets him with a clouded face. His desert has, indeed, blossomed as the rose. May the bloom and fragrance thereof never fade nor lose its sweetness!

www.ingramcontent.com/pod-product-compliance
Lightning Source LLC
Chambersburg PA
CBHW031351170626
46807CB00002B/929